It's Never Too Late for Love

Everyone deserves a fairy tale ending

Marsha Casper Cook

Acknowledgements

A special thank you to my family and friends.

To Robin Surface and my editor, Jeff Fleischer, who are always there for me, thank you for everything.

Chapter One

Noah glanced over toward his phone, deciding whether he should answer it. It was his mother. If he didn't answer, she would keep calling until he did. So, rather than wait for seven more calls, he answered. "Hey, right on time. Just about to order a beef sandwich in your honor."

"Frank's?" she asked.

"Is there another place? Who do you miss more, Frank's or me?"

Rosalyn laughed in her hearty way. "Frank's, of course. Love those beef sandwiches. Wish he'd open in Florida."

"That's never going to happen. He loves cold weather. Chicago's the place for him."

"Not for me. I love the sunshine. I don't miss the bad weather; I just miss you."

"Okay, I know why you called, Mom. It was last night's date. Am I right?"

Rosalyn paused before answering. "Are you mad?"

"Nope, I'm not. Should be, but I'm used to it. She's engaged and getting married in six months. Really, Mom?"

"I'm so sorry. I should have come clean. Ruthie Mankowitz was hoping for a miracle. She doesn't like her granddaughter's pick, and wanted her to marry a doctor. Who knew?"

Noah laughed. "Apparently, she did. Madeline Mankowitz is soon to be wed."

"Okay, no more fix-ups, except for the one on Saturday. Too late to stop the plan. I made a promise, so just do you mom a favor. Just one more."

"Can I take your word on this?"

Rosalyn hated to lie to her son, so she changed the subject. "Vera and Essie say hello. And, just for the record, they made me promise no more fix-ups from sunny Florida on their watch. They told me you'll find someone on you own. Handsome doctors always do."

"You've got two great best friends. That's good advice they gave you."

"I barely know them," Rosalyn joked, just as she was about to say goodbye.

"The three of you live in the same building, and you've known each other since elementary school, but who's counting?"

"Apparently you are," Rosalyn said. "See you when I see you."

"What does that mean?" Noah asked, wondering if she had planned another surprise visit.

In her usual noncommittal way, Rosalyn quickly said goodbye, leaving Noah staring at the phone and wondering if she was going to call back.

She did, one minute later. "Okay, one last thing. Call me after Saturday's date. Unless you're having so much fun that you forget to think of your long-lost mother waiting for a call while she sits by the pool, playing bingo and drinking a piña colada. Bye."

Chapter Two

As Noah expected, that Saturday's date was another disaster. Rather than go home after it, he decided to check out the pet store down the block. Noah enjoyed meeting the new rescue dogs at the store. Besides, he loved seeing his fraternity brother Jordy, who owned the place. It had been a quite a while since he had nothing to do, so he decided to take advantage of the free time.

As he walked into the store, there was a beautiful, white-and-caramel Cavalier King Charles spaniel looking at him. She seemed to be sizing him up as a new owner, and was wagging her tail. Noah's heart melted when he looked into her lonely, large, round eyes. He turned away and she whimpered. Then he smiled and started to imagine himself finally getting a dog. She was licking his hand, and he was petting her beautiful, fleecy head. They were a match.

Jordy could see Noah was eyeing one of his favorite new dogs. "She's a cutie. Just came in this week."

"Great. Can I take her out of the cage?"

"Absolutely. She's very sweet. You'll like her; she's special."

As Noah lifted her up, she looked right into his eyes. He thought it felt a little strange for them to have such a connection. He was superstitious, so he took it as a sign. "How about coming home with me?"

Jordy stroked the little puppy's head. "So, you finally found the right one? Shall we wrap her up?"

"When can I have her?"

"Give me a day and she'll be ready. I just want to have the vet check her out, and then she's yours." They shook hands on the deal.

Noah was so excited to finally get what he wanted. His parents always told him he could buy himself a dog when he grew up, and it was time. He was a little lonely, but he hated to admit it. If he mentioned loneliness to his mother, she would be on the next plane out of Florida, ready to ask everyone she ever knew if they had a single daughter or friend. After all, who wouldn't want their daughter to be fixed up with a doctor? The world was changing, but not Jewish mothers.

Then his phone rang. "Noah, darling, it's your mother."

"I know. You're right on time."

"So, how did it go?"

"Some restaurant you picked," Noah said. "They must not have paid their electric bill. The windows were grimy, and it was dark and dingy — a perfect breeding ground for bacteria."

"What about Janis? What did you think of her?"

"Wonderful. She was perfect in every way."

"Really? She was a good pick?"

"Everything you'd expect or hope for...if I was a woman."

"Meaning?"

"She likes girls."

Rosalyn sighed in disappointment.

"She does. And please, no more fix-ups. Promise me you won't."

"Cross my heart and hope to die. But..."

"You might not want to say that. You're Jewish, remember? I know fixing me up has become a hobby, or more like a full-time job, for you. But no more, please. Mom, have you ever heard of destiny? Maybe my destiny is not marrying. You do know I go out with lots of women?"

"Fine, no more fix-ups." Rosalyn was lying, and Noah knew it.

"Besides, I might have found a girl. She's got big eyes, and she's as cute as could be. Her bronze, shiny hair is a little curly, and the world changes when she smiles. She's perfect in every way." Noah hated lying to his mother, but she left him no choice. He couldn't go on another one of her horrible dates, even if some were just for coffee or tea.

Rosalyn's voice raised in tone. "Really?"

"Yes, really. Next time you come in, you can meet her. In fact, I'm going to see her tomorrow. I'll keep you posted. Love you, Mom. Enjoy the weather and have fun. No need to worry about me. Bye."

After Noah hung up, Rosalyn looked at the phone. She smiled and looked up toward Heaven. "Ben, if you're listening, it's really going to happen. Your son may have found his mate!"

Then she thought about it for a minute, and wondered if he was just telling her that so she would stop trying to find that perfect someone for him. After all, this wasn't a Hallmark movie.

Her friends were there, busily setting up their afternoon card game. It was much too hot to be outside. Playing in the humid air was not exactly what the doctor would order for any of them.

Rosalyn stood there looking at the phone, dying to call Noah back and ask him if he really did find a nice girl. If he did, she would sleep better; if he didn't, she would continue her search. Lately, though, her sources had dried up.

Essie called out to her, "Ready whenever you are."

"Coming."

"So, the date went well?" Essie asked as she started to pull her toward the card table. "Come on, we're not getting any younger."

Essie's sister, Vera, was waiting for them. "So, was it a match?"

"Nope. The date's over. Remind me to spit in Flora's coffee. She could have told me her daughter Janis was gay. That's it for Flora; let's get a replacement for her. She cheats at cards anyway."

Essie gave her a look. "She's your friend, not ours. I told you she lies."

"Anyway, I have an idea. Let's pack and take a trip. Let's go to Chicago. It's too hot here."

"It's too cold there," Vera replied.

"This calls for a serious discussion. I'm not getting any younger, you know. I need to get that boy married off. He needs a wife. Besides, I want grandchildren while I'm young enough to enjoy them."

Vera gave her friend a look. "Give it some time. You're too impatient."

"I don't have time, Vera. Look at my Ben. One, two, three, and he was gone."

Essie chimed in. "One, two, three? It was more like one, two, three, four, five, six. The man had six heart attacks. He wasn't just gone like the wind. It took a little time."

Rosalyn gave them both a look. "Whatever. One or six, what's the difference? He's gone and we're going. My treat. I'll get the tickets. It will be like a mini-vacation."

Vera shook her head. "Vacation? It's not even twenty degrees there."

"I know. Pack a jacket. Oh, and don't forget to pack boots and gloves. Remember, you fell last time."

"Exactly."

"But you didn't break anything," Rosalyn added. "You'll be more careful this time."

"Gee, thanks, Mom. Such concern."

Chapter Three

Noah was eager to pick up his new puppy. He loaded up a shopping cart with books on how to train a dog, how to take care of a dog, how to make sure a dog's health is up to par, and, last but not least, how to name a dog.

That was just for starters. He also bought dog toys, a doggie coat, boots, a leash, and lots of dog food, including treats. He was prepared.

He smiled as Jordy handed her over. "She's a great dog. Enjoy her."

"I'm sure going to try," Noah said, as he held her tightly to his chest. "Well, it's just you and me."

The car ride home was a little tricky, with slick roads and bad traffic, but Noah lucked out. His dog appeared a lot calmer than he was. In fact, every time he looked in the rearview mirror, it seemed as if his new dog was looking right at him. He had never had a dog before, and assumed all dogs reacted the same way. All he knew was he was a nervous wreck. He tried reassuring himself that he could do this.

As soon as they walked in the door, even before he unpacked all the dog supplies, Noah sat on the couch and pulled his new friend up to sit beside him. "Hmm, got to find a great name for you."

He picked up his phone and googled dog names. "Samantha, Jackie, Willow, Ramona, Bella, Flora, Allie, Ellie. Nope. None of these seem like a good fit. Hold everything. Let me get the book."

Without warning, his little dog looked at him and said, "Maybe I can help."

For a moment, Noah thought it was his imagination. "You didn't talk, did you?"

"Sure did."

"Oh my God, I've lost it." Noah was beside himself.

"You haven't. Just hand over the book, and we'll have a name for me in a minute or two. Names are important. Don't you think?"

"I'm not sure what I think. Actually, that's not true; I really think I'm going crazy. My dog is talking to me."

"Don't worry, you'll get used to it."

Noah was silent for a minute or two. "So, I did hear you talk, right?"

"Yep, no denying that. Why don't you fix dinner while I check out some names? And, while you're at it, maybe you should fix yourself a drink. You look a little beat. I hear wine is relaxing."

"You can read?"

"Sure can. Rosetta Stone. Short course."

"Okay, maybe you're right. I'll have a glass of wine. Maybe even two."

"Hey, Noah, even if you drink the entire bottle of wine, you'll find I really do talk and you're not crazy. When you come back, I'll fill you in."

"Okay, I get it. Maybe."

"Just so you know, I can't think great on an empty stomach. If you could put that in your memory bank, it would be a plus."

Noah quietly watched from the doorway as his new dog glanced through the *Name Your Puppy* book. Noah was confused, and thought he might need a vacation. It wasn't possible that he had a dog who could talk. No way; he was a doctor. Although, some of the kids that he took care of believed animals really talk…

"Noah, I can feel your eyes on me. Don't worry; I'm fine. You can go fix dinner. I'm real, not a figment of your imagination."

"Got it. It's good that someone's fine, because clearly I'm not."

There he went again, talking to a dog. Who would believe this? Maybe he didn't have a dog at all. Maybe he was dead, and this was his afterlife. But, when his phone rang and it was his mother, he knew he wasn't dead. She would always be able to find him, no matter what. He knew if he didn't answer, she would keep calling until he did.

"Mom, what's up?" he asked hurriedly. "Got to go in a minute."

"Sick patient?"

"Yes, terribly." He hated lying to her, but sometimes he had to do what he had to do.

"Well, I called your office, and they told me you were home. I thought you were sick. So, you're okay?"

"I'm fine. Better than ever. Let's talk later."

"Just wanted to tell you something…" Rosalyn didn't have a chance to finish. Noah never heard that his mother was leaving for Chicago, or that she'd be there soon.

His dog seemed to be observing his behavior.

"Okay, what is it?" he asked her.

"You shouldn't lie to your mother. You're lucky to have one. Rosalyn loves you."

Oh no, Noah thought. *This couldn't be happening. More guilt.*

"You know Rosalyn? How?"

"Let's put it in the proper perspective."

"Yes, let's."

"After dinner. Okay?"

"Fine."

"I'm kind of hungry. If I may compliment you on your choices, you bought the Cadillac of dog food. I'm impressed."

"And you know that because…"

"Television. I love TV, don't you? Jordy always had a TV going in the pet store. When he left for the day, we all watched."

"You watched TV? All of you watched TV?"

"Not all of us. The cats didn't. They were too busy playing cards."

Noah shook his head in disbelief. "Let's just keep the conversation to a minimum, at least for now. I'm not much of a talker."

"That will change. I can tell you have it in you."

Noah quickly put the food in the dish and brought it out. His dog smelled it before eating. "Just checking. Next time, a little less; I need to keep my girlish figure."

"Okay. If that's what the lady wants, that's what she will get."

"That sounds more like it. See, you're already getting the hang of it. Now back to my name. How about Gracie?"

Noah shrugged his shoulders. "How about Bella? Or Maggie?"

"One of the dogs at the store was named Gracie. It's a good, solid name. On the spiritual side, girls named Gracie like to investigate the unknown and use their mental abilities to find the meaning of life. Shall I go on?"

"How do you know that?"

"I did some research."

"Of course you did. My mistake."

"No problem. So, do you like the name?"

"I'm guessing you do."

"I love that name. It's perfect for me."

Noah just stood there with his mouth wide open.

"I should clue you in," the dog continued. "I'm pretty sure no one else can hear me, but I'm not positive on that point. You'll get used to it, or you can return me — but it would be better for you, and for me, if you gave me a chance to prove myself."

"I'm not returning you like a pair of shoes. I picked you out — or maybe you picked me. It doesn't matter; you're not going anywhere."

"Fair enough, my friend. You'll learn to like me."

Noah smiled, realizing he already did. "Okay, then. Gracie it is. I can live with that. Didn't you mention we would talk about you knowing my mother?"

"We have plenty of time to talk about that."

Gracie closed the book and smiled. As she looked around, she knew she would be happy there. All the conveniences she asked for, a good guy, a wonderful place to live — oh, and a big-screen TV. She thought Noah could have been more organized, but she had heard about single guys and their apartments. She would put that on her to-do list.

Chapter Four

At six in the morning, Noah's alarm clock rang. He almost forgot about Gracie, until she jumped on his bed holding the remote in her mouth.

"Guess you want me to turn it on," he said. Noah made sure Gracie didn't get too close; he needed his space. That might be one reason he was still single, but not the only one. Medical school required a lot of work, and so did working as a doctor. Having a woman in his life would have made it too difficult. There were always dates, but nothing significant.

"Noah, please, no news. I get too stressed."

"It's your house, too, but I like the news. In fact, that's usually the only thing I watch. Though I do watch a movie or two on occasion."

"Okay. I have all day to watch my favorites. So, I'll catch up when you're at work, and at night you can watch whatever you want. I'm glad you have on-demand TV; it's a life saver."

"You have favorites?" Noah asked with sheer surprise. "Favorites? Wow. This is happening, isn't it?"

Gracie didn't want to slobber him with kisses, since she sensed a little apprehension. She didn't like making waves, so she kept her distance and then curled up on the edge of his bed, understanding it might take him some time to warm up. She would turn him around.

"Noah, just so you know, I'm very opinionated, but you'll get used to it." Gracie knew she had her work cut out for her. A request had been made, and she was there to fill it. She wasn't sure when, or if, she should tell Noah why she was there. Would he even want to know? *I'll revisit that thought a little later*, Gracie decided.

Noah turned on the news and sat back against the headboard, watching Gracie. He smiled, thinking it was pretty good to have someone there. *I should have gotten a dog years ago*, he thought. *Well, you know what they say. It's never too late.*

For breakfast, Noah did exactly what Jordy had instructed as far as taking care of Gracie's nutrition. He made sure she had water and a little bit of food — not too much at first — and decided he would try to come home in the middle of the day, so she wouldn't feel abandoned.

He phoned his office to make sure that his schedule was open at lunchtime. But, when he looked into Gracie's eyes, he decided to take her with him. He couldn't leave her. Not yet. Maybe tomorrow.

"Okay, my friend, we're going to work."

"How about calling me Gracie?"

"Fine, Gracie, I have an extra examination room that we can use. You don't seem to bark. No one will even notice you. Can you bark?"

Gracie looked at him. "Would you like it if one of your new patients said to you, 'You don't look like a doctor, hope you know what you're doing?'"

"Actually, I have heard that before. That goes with the territory."

Noah usually didn't like to be challenged as much as Gracie was doing, but for some reason he didn't mind. He didn't understand any of this, but he was too superstitious to question it.

"Noah, do you always think over everything you do a million times? Haven't you ever done anything adventurous? Like spur of the moment?"

"Yes, actually. I have. I brought you home."

"Touché."

That was the last word either of them said before they got down to the garage. They were equally matched.

"So, Noah, how long is the ride? I forgot to mention I get car sick."

Noah took a look at her through the rearview mirror. She seemed a little unhappy. "Take a few deep breaths."

"Thanks, Doc. I needed that."

Oh my God, I'm still talking to a dog, he thought. *Note to me, I'm probably going crazy.*

"Noah, you're not crazy."

"So, you can read my mind too?"

"Sometimes. This might be bad news for you, but you're not that hard to read. You're very expressive, my friend."

Chapter Five

When Noah arrived at the office with Gracie, Annie Porter, his nurse practitioner, had everything ready.

Noah was impressed. "How did you know?"

She laughed. "Because I have a dog, and I know no one wants to leave them alone the first few days. It's lucky you're not working for someone else. They still haven't created a bring-your-dog-to-work day."

"That's true."

"I doubt any landlord would approve of a doctor's office having a dog visit, but since you own the building, we don't have that problem."

Annie had placed a bowl of water and some newspaper on the floor of the extra exam room, just in case of an accident. She even had a few toys and some dog treats for Gracie.

Annie was always spot on for everyone's needs. The office ran smoothly because of her. Noah liked order, but he also knew he lacked certain qualities that Annie possessed, so he left all office activities in her hands. His father had trusted Annie to keep everyone organized, and so did Noah.

"Well, before you get too comfortable, we do have a few issues that need to be attended to," Annie said. "The coffee machine is broken, and the bathroom is a bit of a mess."

"What does that have to do with me?"

"You're a lot better at this than I am. Here you go, Doc," Annie added as she handed him the plunger.

"They didn't teach this in medical school."

Charlotte, the office manager, walked in. "Morning, Doc...whoops!" she said as she took the plunger and went on her merry way. "I've got you covered. Remember how much it cost last time you tried to play handyman?"

Noah laughed. "I do indeed. What a mess. Let's give her a raise."

Annie was laughing. "Not that I don't love her, but she just got one. She painted the office and fixed the bathroom tile. All the cracks. This building isn't exactly new, but she gets the job done."

"Annie, you think of everything."

"Do you really think so?"

"I do. I'm not sure what I would do without you."

"Bet you say that to all the girls."

Noah smiled and walked out, mumbling to himself. "No, not really." Then he turned around and walked back in. "Annie, have I given you a raise?"

"Yes, a nice one." She laughed. "Remember? Three years ago."

"That's not true, is it?"

"I think it was before you got your first gray hair."

"I have a gray hair?"

"Not anymore," she said, as she plucked it out. "I'm just kidding. I give myself a raise every year."

"Good. Keep up the good work."

"I intend too, unless you fire me."

"Don't even kid around about that. This office runs because you're here."

Annie was a little surprised at his comment. She had begun to feel like just another fixture there. She felt a blush come to her face, so she changed the subject. She bent down and hugged Gracie. "How cute is she?"

"I know I shouldn't have brought her, but I just didn't have the heart to leave her alone. No one will know. She rarely barks."

Noah thought to himself that Gracie didn't need to bark, because she talked. But, before that thought fully entered his mind, his quiet-as-a-mouse Gracie started to bark.

Annie smiled. "Guess you don't know her that well. Let's try not to worry and get the day going. We're running behind, but we can catch up."

Charlotte was a little out of breath when she returned. "Now it's time for my coffee."

Annie regretfully looked her way. "Our machine is kaput, and I know you need your coffee. Call the service and see how fast they can bring another one out."

"No worries. I'll take a break soon and run to Starbucks. I like their coffee better anyway." Charlotte looked down and noticed Gracie. "So, you're the one who stole Noah's heart. And they said it couldn't be done."

Noah laughed. "Charlotte, the only one who has ever stolen my heart was you. Charlotte, meet Gracie."

Her laugh was hearty. "If you don't watch out, you could be my sixth husband. I'm available."

"I'm too boring for you. And, by the way, who's answering the phones?" Noah asked.

"I bet you think I put the phones on service. I didn't. Mavis Lawrence kindly offered."

Annie was laughing. "You asked the mailwoman to answer our phones?"

"She didn't mind; she's done it before. She's actually very good at it."

Noah smiled. "Is she also on the payroll?"

Annie laughed. "No, not yet."

"Okay ladies, not that I want to be a killjoy, but I'd better start seeing my patients. Annie, which room first?"

"I think you'd better start in room three. So far, no one has complained, except for Mrs. Bell. She's sure her son has an ear infection again, even though his ear doesn't hurt. But it's Monday, and she's here with Randy, her little angel."

"Anything else I should know?"

"I took his crayons away and brought him a book."

"He'll grow out of it." Noah laughed. "These walls have had a lot of artists showing their talent. I happen to be one of them. My mother still reminds me about how I decorated the office with a marker when I was little, and I guess I grew up despite it." Noah took his stethoscope from his pocket and hung it loosely from his neck. "I've got this."

Annie straightened his collar. "I know you do." Then she offered him a shy, but cautious, smile, realizing she might have overstepped.

Noah was both surprised and intrigued at her unexpected show of affection. It was as if he was seeing her for the first time. He noticed her bangs were slightly covering her eyes, but he could still see the brightness and confidence in her polished style.

He didn't know much about her personal life, but Annie was a terrific practitioner. She may have been petite, but Annie was a powerhouse who kept everyone on their toes. The office staff loved her, and so did the patients. How was it that he never noticed how cute she was?

He felt something, but wasn't sure what that meant; they had known each other for so long. He knew one thing — he couldn't run his office without her. *On my list*, he thought. *Get to know Annie better.*

Annie noticed he was watching her intently. He had never done that before, and she wondered what had brought it on. When she fixed his collar, she was only trying to be helpful, but the tingling in the pit of her stomach said something else. So did her quick pulse. His stare was exhilarating.

Charlotte pulled Annie aside. "You're getting brave."

"What are you talking about?"

"You straightened out Noah's collar."

"So? I've done it before."

"By the look on his face, you haven't. He looked surprised. And I never saw you touch him. Good for you, girl."

"Was it a pleasant surprise or an unwelcome surprise? Did he smile?"

"I think he did, but don't ask me. After five marriages, I haven't got it right yet. I still can't read men."

Annie was always amused by Charlotte's' wit. "Oh, well, it was nothing."

The day passed quickly, although they had few incidents, which wasn't bad for a Monday. A couple of wild ones ran down the hall, and two threw up. One little one took out all the supplies in the drawers, opened every box and Band-Aid, and tossed everything in the air. His father was a child psychologist; so much for at-home training.

Just before the day was over, Noah made it into the lounge, where Annie and Charlotte were chatting and having a cup of coffee. They thought Gracie was taking a nap, but was she was soaking up the entire conversation. She found it enlightening, to say the least.

"I see we now have coffee again." Noah smiled, looking forward to the night. "One problem solved."

Charlotte lifted her cup. "Thank goodness for coffee. Without it, I wouldn't have this perfect figure." Then she laughed, realizing she had gained a few pounds. Twenty, to be exact. She loved anything from Starbucks, but when she asked for whipped cream and chocolate, that made it so much better. For her, something sugary took the place of a man when she was between lovers.

Noah thought for a moment, then moved a little closer to the girls. "Annie, before I leave, do you think you can join me tonight? There are some guys I'd like you to meet."

Annie gave him a serious look. "I'm not interested in a fix-up. I'd say you have had enough fix-ups to cover all of us in this office."

Charlotte laughed. "Got any guys for me to meet? I need one of those old guys with a lot of money and a hefty insurance policy. One who loves to give expensive jewelry to his woman. Oh, and one who can drive at night and see over the steering wheel. Also, one who can cook, clean, and still fulfill me with wonderful bedroom pleasures."

Annie smiled. "That's a little over the top, don't you think? One too many requests."

"Well, let's put it this way — five men couldn't satisfy me."

Noah laughed. "Annie, it's not a fix-up. Promise. Can you come?"

"Sure. I have nothing planned. Just me and Molly."

"Who's Molly?"

"She's my dog. I rescued her a few years ago."

"Oh. Nice. I didn't know…I should have, shouldn't I? Sorry."

"Yes, dear," Charlotte added. "You should have."

"So, you'll go?" he repeated.

"Can't stay out late," Annie said.

"No problem. I promise."

"Okay, give me a few minutes."

"Sure, but I need to be there at six."

Annie nodded, watching Noah and Gracie walk toward another room.

"You're coming, too," Noah whispered to Gracie once they were far enough away from the others.

"You know I missed my shows today," Gracie whispered. "Tonight, my favorite is on. I love *Dancing with the Stars*."

Noah didn't say another word. He just stared at Gracie, not quite sure what to make of this whole talking-doggie experience.

Annie thought it was sweet to see Noah enjoying his new dog. He seemed a little more relaxed than usual. She couldn't help but wonder why he picked that night to take her somewhere. Whatever the reason, she was glad to go. She rarely went out.

Noah was aware she was watching him, so he decided to finish his conversation with Gracie in the car. Gracie sighed in relief. "Can I stay home tomorrow?"

"Yep. I got you a dog walker."

"Really? Do you know who it is? Aren't you afraid they might take me and never bring me back? Don't you know there are a lot of bad people out there?"

"Actually, Annie offered. She goes home during lunch, and you're on the way."

Gracie took a deep breath, thinking this was a perfect way to map out a plan. "You know, Noah, you're lucky to have someone like Annie. Looks like she takes pretty good care of you."

Noah smiled. "I think you might be right. I never really noticed."

"I picked up on that," Gracie added.

Chapter Six

It was a short ride, and Noah didn't say where they were going. When Annie got in, however, things changed. Noah was lively and very relaxed talking to her.

All good signs, Gracie thought.

"Noah, the suspense is killing me," Annie said, still wondering why she was asked to go.

"Okay, maybe I should explain. I'm a part-time coach for a Special Olympics team from Midtown School. I've been teaching nine young teens to play basketball. All the guys have special needs, but they wanted to play. I'm on the board of the school, so I offered to coach. I love basketball, and I couldn't be happier. It's one of the best things I've ever done."

"I had no idea. That's wonderful. Lucky guys. I bet your mother is thrilled."

"She doesn't know."

"Why not?"

"You know my mother's obsessed with me getting married. That's her only goal, and I'm not exactly making it easy on her. I guess I could have tried harder, but I don't know, that's not what love is about for me. I just pretend to like someone, only to make her happy. In the long run, that's not the way to happiness."

"Noah, have you ever thought that's the only way she knows? She loves you, and she wants you to be happy."

"I know that, but I can't just snap my fingers and say, 'She's the one' if she's not. That would be horrible."

"She just thinks that's the best thing for you."

"I like my life the way it is. Maybe marriage isn't for me. Is that such a bad thing?"

"No, of course not, but it would make her happy to see you well on your way to having your own family."

Noah looked over toward Annie. "You seem happy enough, and you're not married."

"Don't use me for an example. I just wake up in the morning, go to work, go home, and go to sleep. Every day is pretty much the same. Mine might not be a dream life for anyone."

"You must have lots of dates. I see the divorced fathers eyeing you when they're in the office."

"Noah, don't tell me you notice that."

"Well, I'm human. I just assumed some of them got your attention."

"I have a rule against dating patients. My workplace is not a personal haven for picking up guys." Then she laughed. "Not my style."

"I didn't mean that. Sorry."

"No apology needed. Look at you. I have seen many starry-eyed moms looking at you."

"You're kidding. I've never noticed. Guess I'm too busy taking care of their kids."

"Well, now you know."

Noah was a little surprised that Annie didn't have a full social calendar. "I hope you don't hold it against me for talking about the dads."

"I didn't think you noticed."

Noah smiled as he turned on the radio. "Let's liven this party up."

Gracie's ears perked up. She was shocked that Noah liked pop music.

"Anyway, thanks for bringing me tonight," Annie said. "Thank goodness you're not trying to fix me up. I hate fix-ups."

"Me too," Noah said. "Why would you think I would do that to you?"

"I don't know. When you said, 'Meet the guys,' I thought…never mind. I'm looking forward to this."

"My mother thinks that's the only way, but I don't think like that."

"Good to know." Annie was happy.

Noah questioned himself. *Why would I do that to her? Damn, then I would lose her.* He didn't quite understand what was happening to him. *A few days ago, I didn't have a dog, and I hadn't even thought of Annie as someone to go out with.*

He was glad they had finally arrived at the school. The traffic was heavy, and the streets were slick. The news reports were right; severe weather was on the way. It was good that they left the office early, before the snow. Noah didn't want to be late and keep the kids waiting.

Noah's team greeted them in a loud, fun-loving way. The guys surrounded him with a big group bear hug, and then they circled around Gracie. "Noah, who's this? Hi, Noah's friend."

Noah smiled. "Yes, introductions. Annie, meet my favorite guys in the whole wide world. My team."

Mark, one of the boys, smiled. "Noah has a girlfriend. Woah! Noah, she's pretty. Very pretty."

One of the other guys, Andrew, put out his hand for her to shake. "Annie, hi." Without anyone coaxing them, the rest of the boys were right there, shaking hands with Annie.

Annie reciprocated and smiled. "So nice to meet you. You've got yourself a good coach. Dr. Meyers is the best."

Another boy, Alex, was a regular patient. He was so happy to see Annie. "Annie's my nurse! She works with Noah. Right, Annie?"

"Yes, sir," she said. "Nice to see you, Alex."

"Guys, also meet my new dog, Gracie," Noah continued. "She'll be coming with me to all the practices."

Noah's team seemed thrilled to meet Annie and Gracie, but Noah knew he had limited time with the guys. He promised their parents it wouldn't be a long meeting, and he didn't like to go back on his word. They had busy lives, but knew that Noah was trying to make a difference for the kids.

"Okay guys," Noah said, as he opened his gym bag and took out t-shirts. "Here they are. Just in time for the first game." Noah unwrapped the shirts and handed one to each of the kids. "I promised you would have them, so put them on. We need to hurry up and see if they fit. Let's not get your parents mad at me; we don't have many days left until showtime."

Annie had a wonderful reaction as she looked around. Her feelings for Noah were growing stronger, but she had very little experience with men.

Her good friend Wesley was the only one she really opened up to about Noah. Wes lived in her building and was a little shy, but not with Annie. He was gay, but somehow his mom always hoped Annie could win his heart. That was obviously never going to happen, though he was sweet and very handsome, with curly, blonde hair and big, blue eyes.

They spent holidays together, which made his family happy. Annie had told Wes more than once about how she hoped Noah might see her as she saw him. Now, finally spending time with Noah outside the office, she was one step closer than yesterday.

Noah was patient with the kids, and they seemed so relieved to act just as they were. Annie was both fascinated and thrilled to watch Noah interact with them. She knew why she had fallen in love with him; his kindness was shining through.

The kids were cheering as they came running out with their new shirts on. Noah applauded as he watched them come on the court. They looked great, and the smiles on their faces made everything worthwhile. Noah was a happy man, and it showed.

"Listen up, guys."

All nine of them listened. As Annie watched the team and Noah, she was so happy to be a part of this.

"Now that we have our wardrobe problem solved, you guys need to go home and get some rest. Tomorrow's a school day. Don't forget, we're going to practice this weekend, because we don't have much time before the big game."

Noah was always happy to see their smiles. "Okay, listen up. We know winning isn't everything, right?"

All at once, they shouted, "Yes, we know that. But…"

One of the guys, Casey, looked up at him. "What if we don't do good?"

Noah could tell they were nervous. "Sitting on the sidelines is never good. Just do your best. Numbers don't matter. We're still going to have our pizza party. Win or lose, it's about having fun. Now, let's finish up fast with our huddle, so your parents won't be mad. We're running late, and most of them are lined up waiting in the parking lot, but we still need our hugs."

All nine of them shouted out, "Yay, team us! Yay Heroes!"

Noah waved the team on. "All for one and one for all!" Then they jumped up and down, and clapped their hands high in the air.

As the boys were running out, Noah ran toward Annie and gave her a big hug. Gracie watched, taking it all in. *Cute couple*, she thought. *Looks like they were made for each other.*

"Annie, what do you think of my guys? Aren't they great?"

"Noah, you never cease to amaze me. Thanks so much for sharing this evening with me. It was terrific. They love you, and it's wonderful to watch. Their happy faces tell it all."

Noah smiled. "And to think they want to close this school."

"You're kidding. Why?"

"I wish I were. We're not getting the donations we need to keep it open. Private schools are closing left and right. I just don't want to let the kids down. We need funding to help us continue."

"I'm sure something will come up. You'll figure out a way."

"Maybe the money will fall from the sky — we need a miracle." Noah shook his head, realizing he might not be on the list. He could only hope.

"Miracles do happen," Annie added with optimism.

She was always there, cheering him on. Noah liked that about her, but never told her. He wondered why he didn't compliment her more.

"I hope you're right," he said. "I don't want to let these kids down."

"You won't."

"Hey, how about dinner? You must be hungry by now."

"I can't. Sorry. I don't like to be out this late. Molly's used to me coming home right after work, and I need to feed her and let her out. We're company for each other. You'll understand when you have Gracie a little longer."

"I'm already getting used to her being around. It's kind of nice. Anyway, how about a raincheck?"

Noah seemed disappointed, so Annie took a leap of faith. "Hey, why don't you let me fix dinner? Gracie's already with you and Molly's alone, so come over. It will be fun."

"Sounds like a plan. I think I would like that."

"Great. I'm a good cook."

"And I'm not, so I accept." Noah laughed. "I'm starved, and I do get tired of takeout. Love home cooking."

Annie was a little overwhelmed. She decided it was pretty brave of her to ask. *More importantly*, she thought, *he said yes*.

They were both a little quiet in the car, but that was to be expected, as neither of them had planned this day. Annie had thought often about Noah coming over for dinner, but she never asked. She was always afraid he would say no.

From the moment they met years ago, she had always liked Noah. As the years passed, she liked him that much more. She started in his father's office as a file clerk, then went to nursing school, and become a nurse practitioner. She would be forever grateful to Ben Meyers, Noah's father, for paying her tuition and helping her achieve her goals.

Annie didn't have her own family — her parents had died when she was little — so Ben and Rosalyn Meyers were all she had. Noah had no idea how many wonderful things his parents did for her, but Annie held all those memories close to her heart. She owed them everything.

Chapter Seven

When they got to Annie's apartment, Molly, a beautiful golden retriever, was waiting at the door.

Noah bent down and hugged her. "Hi, girl. She's a beauty. How long have you had her?"

"A little over two years. It's been terrific having her around." Not liking to talk about herself, Annie quickly shifted the conversation. "How about some wine?"

"Great. I'd like that."

After they settled in, Annie brought out two glasses and a bottle wine. "Noah, will you do the honors?"

While Noah poured, he couldn't help but notice how many gadgets she had in her kitchen. He tried not to stare, but couldn't help it.

"Bet you didn't know I could cook," she said, acknowledging that he was examining her surroundings.

"I had no idea, but it looks like you have every utensil ever made. Not that I know that much about cooking, but it seems as though you're ready for any occasion."

"Almost. I love fooling around in the kitchen, making up new recipes and having fun reinventing what others have done in the past. It's like a game to me."

"Good for you. I wish I had a hobby."

"You do. You enjoy coaching the kids at the school."

"Never thought of it that way. All I know is I love it."

"Do you want to stay in the kitchen, or go in the study and watch TV while I get dinner ready?"

"I'll stay in here, if that's okay. Maybe I can help, or even learn something. I wish I could cook. My mom's great at it, as you know. She tried to teach me years ago, but I never got the hang of it."

She started to pull out vegetables from the fridge and seasonings from the cabinets. The clean counters were soon covered with jars and sauces. Noah couldn't help but notice how much she was enjoying herself. He was having fun watching her and, at the same time, wondering why had he had not done this before. He was trying not to be too inquisitive, but she was very entertaining. "This is like watching the food shows."

"Noah, you're kidding me, right? You watch cooking shows?"

"Can I plead the Fifth?"

"Come on. I won't laugh or anything like that. So, do you?"

"I don't watch much TV, but cooking intrigues me. I watch, but never really try anything. It makes me hungry, and then I eat."

"Sounds fascinating," she said, as she tossed him a bag of carrots. "Okay, lesson number one. It's your time to shine, Chef Meyers."

"I might need assistance. I can do sutures, but as for cooking, we'll see."

"Okay, here you go," she said, as she handed him a knife and a few jars of seasoning. "You can do this. Improvise Think of it as a science experiment."

"I'll give it a try." He placed the carrots on a cutting board, after drenching them with a little too much water. It looked as if he was drowning the carrots, rather than washing them. They were shriveling, and not very appealing. "Cooking might not be my thing," he said, surrendering the knife. "Better stick to suturing."

"You can't give up that fast."

He smiled. "Will there be a lesson two?"

"That all depends on you, Doctor." She took a quiet breath. She was nervous, and wondered how she got to be so bold.

As Noah looked around her kitchen, he was a little surprised at how everything was labeled and categorized. That was how Annie ran his office, but he wasn't expecting her own apartment to be so systematically designed. "You must have lots of guests."

"Actually, no. As you know, I work a lot."

"True. Me too."

"Just like you watch cooking shows, my secret is I watch a lot of the home-shopping shows. It's such fun." What she didn't say was she watched them because they made her feel like she was part of something. It was lonely living alone. Her life did change when she rescued Molly, but it probably wasn't enough.

While Gracie was observing their interactions, she couldn't help but notice how uncomfortable both Noah and Annie were. *What a challenge this is going to be*, she thought, *and they have known each other for years.* All she needed was for them to realize they were made for each other.

"Noah, how about that wine now?"

"Wine sounds great. What shall we toast to?"

"Tomorrow. Let's hope we don't have a snowstorm."

"How about to more evenings like this?"

She nearly spat out the wine. Now she was getting nervous.

Noah was not that good with small talk, but Annie excelled at it. He knew that about her. Annie was the queen of chitchat; that was part of why all their patients loved her. She made everyone feel as if they were the most important person in the world. Noah often listened to her conversations, admiring that about her, but he never told her.

It was obvious to Gracie that Annie was trying not to touch Noah or get too close to him, and he was doing the same.

Childish, she thought. *These two really need some help with their romantic skills. That must be why I'm here, but this isn't going to be easy. Then again, what is?* Gracie continued to watch, silently taking notes in her head.

Then, as clear as day, Noah took his own leap of faith. "Annie, I might not be an expert in social graces, but there's something I have wanted to do all evening."

Annie had no idea what he meant, but suddenly found his arms around her. The water was still running in the kitchen sink, but neither of them seemed to care. It wasn't the most romantic atmosphere, but that didn't matter.

Noah placed his lips gently on hers. His kiss was slow and thoughtful. Her lips were more persuasive than she cared to admit. For years, she had imagined what it would feel like, but nothing could have prepared her for the sweetness of his kiss. She breathed lightly between her parted lips, and was shocked as her passion rose. The kiss was perfect.

For a moment, their eyes did not sway from each other. Noah was stunned by the lingering effect of just one kiss. Annie felt her legs quiver, almost giving way. Just as she was about to speak, the water from the sink began to flow to the floor.

"Oh my God, the water's on." Annie quickly grabbed some dishtowels from a drawer. "Oh shit, it's everywhere."

They both anxiously laughed as they tended to the flood happening before their eyes. Water was coming from all sides.

Gracie watched thinking, *What a kiss. It's like the sea parted. Didn't think these two were that powerful. Wow, now that was soap-opera quality.*

After they cleaned up the water, there was a silence between them, each focusing on their own memory of what just took place. Annie sipped her wine with a lingering grin. Noah, always reserved, loosened up a bit with a faint smile as he thought about what happened in replay. He was a little more aggressive with his drink, gulping it down in one second flat. "So, now that we got that out of the way, we can enjoy the evening."

Annie smiled. "I think we should definitely enjoy the evening. Might not be a such a good idea to have any more wine."

Noah laughed. "You might be right, considering we have to go to work tomorrow."

Now the clumsiness of their being together became less noticeable. Gracie lay back on the floor and closed her eyes. *Nothing too exciting is going to happen here*, she thought.

While Noah was taking a call, Annie answered a knock at her door. She would have liked to ignore it, but she didn't.

It was Wes, her neighbor and confidant. He was about to walk in, but Annie motioned to him that she had a guest. Wes wasn't getting the message, so Annie had to whisper. "Do you think you could come back tomorrow? I'm a little busy right now."

"Oh, I get it," he said. "You have a guy here."

She nodded and smiled.

"I'd like to meet the man of the hour. Just a peek?"

"Nope. I'll fill you in later," she whispered to him. "Not just any guy. It's Noah."

"Well, as I live and breathe. The doctor is in the house."

With a few subtle pushes, she moved him out into the hall. "I'll let you know how it goes later."

"No can do. I'm going out on the town with my new guy. Just met him this afternoon. He's a hottie."

"Wes, how about this? Why don't we have dinner tomorrow? I'll make all your favorites."

"Honey, not good enough. You know how nosy I am. Please. Pretty please. I want to meet the guy who's got your heart."

"Banana cake for a month."

"Bingo." He smiled, kissed her on the cheek, and left.

Just as she closed the door, Noah asked, "Neighbor?"

She smiled. "Yes, a neighbor friend." Wes was really more like a brother. They had been friends from the first day she moved in. She needed help hanging some pictures and, after the moving truck pulled away, Wes appeared with a hammer and a goody bag filled with food. Every picture was carefully placed and secured, except for the one she hung; it fell twice, and the glass cracked on the third attempt.

It was an instant friendship. Wes was such fun, and Annie was thrilled to have someone to share good and tough times with, without the pressures of a relationship. She was saving herself for Noah, and Wes was really the only person she trusted enough to share her secret.

"Is everything okay?" she asked. "Must be tough being on call all the time."

"It's not too bad; I'm used to it. It was just the service. Janie Robbins lost the prescription I wrote today. I knew I should have called it in."

"Well, what about dinner?" Annie asked.

"I'm starved," Noah said. "Maybe the wine without eating was a little too much for both of us."

"You're right. I never have more than one or two sips, and tonight...well, you know what I mean."

"I do. The kiss, right?"

"Yep, the kiss. Noah we've known each other too long, so maybe I'd better come clean."

"I'm listening. Hope you're not mad or uncomfortable. I know it was impulsive. But, it was kind of nice. Don't you think?"

"Yes, it was pretty damn wonderful." She knew the wine was talking; she wouldn't have been so brave without it.

Their evening was progressing well. They began to joke and converse, as if to erase the self-conscious feeling they both had earlier.

It was late when they finally finished dinner, and Noah was shocked when he peeked outside. A lot of snow had fallen since they got there; it was practically a blizzard. "Maybe they're waiting for the snow to stop," he said as he closed the blinds, "because it doesn't look as if a plow has hit the street yet."

"You can always stay here on the couch." She was kidding, she thought…but maybe she wasn't.

"I'll leave in a little while."

Noah had another glass of wine, and so did Annie. She usually had a limit of one glass, but that night Annie went a little over her usual intake. She was trying her best not to say anything she would regret. (Nothing like, "I love you, Noah, and always have," or "Kiss me again," or "You really can stay here tonight, but I'm afraid it will ruin our friendship.") She decided the less she talked about the kiss, the better. Her lips were now sealed.

"You know, Annie, tonight has been fun. I do have one question. Why is it that you know so much more about me than I do about you?"

"That's because your father was so proud of you. You were his favorite subject, and I listened. Not only was he a great doctor, but he was a good father."

Noah grinned. "Yes, he was."

"I could tell, because he supported you in everything you did. He was certain you would be a good doctor, and he was right."

A little embarrassed, Noah didn't know what to say. "You probably got sick of hearing about my boring life story. I'm not that interesting."

Annie smiled as she looked over toward him with all sincerity. "You're very interesting. Besides, I always wished I had a father who loved me. I thought it was really nice for a father to care so much."

He kept seeing things about Annie that he really liked, and wondered why he had never seen any of this before. Was he too self-absorbed?

"Noah, why are you looking at me that way?"

"No reason. I was just thinking of how nice you are, and why it took us so long to talk like this. We're with each other almost every day."

"We are, but we're usually surrounded by crying children and nervous moms. That's our job."

Noah laughed. "That's true, but for the first time in a long time, I'm really feeling relaxed. I don't want it to end."

Annie sat there, speechless.

"Are you uncomfortable?" Noah asked, sensing a little anxiety.

"A tiny bit, but I'll get over it."

"It's just been an overall great night. I haven't had such an open and honest conversation in many,

many...scratch that. I've never had a conversation like this. As you know, I've had my share of dates, but tonight is different. At least it is for me."

"So, this is a date?" Annie nervously asked, shrugging it off as idle talk. "I suppose it is. And, if I might add, a good one."

They both laughed, realizing something unusual was happening. "Sorry, Annie, didn't mean for you to feel funny about us having a little alone time."

"Noah, I'm really enjoying tonight, too, but..."

"Is this the time you tell me that there's someone else?"

Annie couldn't help but laugh.

"What's so funny?"

"Noah, there is no one else. I'm pretty much an open book. Like I said before, I work all day, come home, have dinner, and then I get up and go to work again."

Noah was surprised by their similarities. "That sounds like my life, except for the fact that my mother usually has a date or two planned. Which you usually hear about the next day."

"Love those stories."

"In the scheme of things, you and I have been so busy trying to get my practice going that nothing else seemed to matter. You've helped me more than you could ever know."

Annie was speechless. She was puzzled by his behavior, because she always thought he didn't notice anything she did, but she was flattered to realize he knew she was there for him. Maybe she wasn't just Annie from the office.

Gracie didn't take her eyes off them. *Geez, these two really like each other, but they're so damn stiff,* she thought. *Loosen up, guys.*

As they sat across from each other, Noah couldn't help but notice how beautiful Annie was. Her features were dainty, and her short, brown hair framed her adorable face. Her lashes were long, and very dark. Her complexion was snowy, with a rosy tint to her cheeks, and her eyes were glowing.

She had the sweetest smile, and he couldn't help but join her when she laughed. Noah realized he didn't laugh very often, but Annie had made it very difficult not to, and she had a wonderful sense of humor. Noah knew he was staring, but he couldn't seem to take his eyes from hers.

Annie didn't have to stare at him; she knew his attributes like the back of her hand. His dark eyes stood out in his handsome face, and his profile was strong and rigid. His features were very sensual, and hard to resist. Many times, she had closed her eyes and wondered what it would be like to be kissed by him, but she didn't expect that it would ever happen. Now, at least, she didn't need to wonder.

Annie kept looking over toward Gracie, but the dog pretended to be asleep. Gracie would have liked to see another kiss or two, but it didn't look like the evening would turn out that way. *Looks like romance is not either of their specialty*, Gracie thought. *Too bad. They need help. Lots of it.*

"Tell me more about you," Noah said.

"Not much to say. As you know, your parents were so kind to me when I was a young girl. Things could have turned out so differently if I didn't have guidance. Your dad gave me that, and your mother's advice taught me things no one else would have."

"They told me some things, but just generalities. They were usually private about most issues other than me. That's why everyone seems to know the details of my love life, which really should be irrelevant to most people. Not that you could tell from my mother's constant search for a princess for her Jewish prince. She knows I'm not thrilled about her search."

"You know she does it out of love."

"I do, but never mind about me. I really do want to know you better."

"My father died when I was a baby, and I never knew him. Then, shortly after I started school, my mother got very ill and sent me to live with her cousin. Believe it or not, after she passed away, my mother's loving cousin sent me to an orphanage — because if my mother was gone, she didn't have to do the right thing. There was no one else who would take me in. So, that about does it for my early years."

Noah was slightly taken aback. "I had no idea. I'm so sorry."

"Your father was terrific to all of us with no family ties. After all, as you know, older kids aren't usually the ones who get adopted."

"All too well. Unfortunately, I know one too many parents who can't accept their children's challenges, and don't. They are pretty damn selfish. That's one of the reasons I love coaching the boys. Some of them have had more than a few tough breaks."

"Your dad used to visit the orphanage every month for checkups for all of us. He wanted us to be up on our immunizations, and always talked to us to make sure we were doing okay."

"Wow. I didn't know all this."

"There were many times when your father brought your mother. She used to talk to a few of us older girls and advise us if we had questions about anything. She was always patient and understanding. You know how they say girls need their mother? Well, that's true, but Rosalyn was there for us. We had some great talks, and that was so helpful to me. Sometimes, your mom brought us ice cream and chocolate-chip cookies. We all loved the time she spent with us."

"Sounds like her. Good old Rosalyn. She used to pack my lunch with the best snacks, and all the guys at my lunch table wished they had a mom like mine."

"Also, your dad was such a good man. You're just like him."

Noah's face flushed a shade of crimson. "I didn't think I was anything like him, but it does feel good to be compared to him."

Gracie perked up. *Now we're getting somewhere*, she thought.

"I don't know if you realize how much those kids on your team love you. I could see it in each and every one's eyes. Not to mention how happy their parents must be."

"Thanks. I try."

"You're taking such an interest in helping their children. Of course they're happy."

"I hope so, because it's actually the best part of my week. I'm so glad to do it."

"You need to tell your mother. She would be so proud. I think this would be something any mother would want to know."

"Even mine?"

"Especially yours. Your mother thinks you're terrific, which is so sweet. You're lucky to have parents who cared about you. Your mom's a cutie. She just wants the best for you."

"I know that, but those dates she fixes me up with — they're bad, really bad. Getting married doesn't mean everything in your life will be perfect. I like my life."

Annie and Noah both laughed. Gracie shook her head, wanting to speak up and tell Noah to kiss her again.

"Okay, Annie," Noah said, "weren't we supposed to be talking about you? Tell me more."

"I'm really not that interesting."

"Why don't you let me make that decision? From what I can see, you're pretty fascinating."

Now, it was Annie's turn to blush. "Okay. I love ice cream, cookies, and candy. They're not exactly healthy foods, but I'm not perfect. When I cook, it's healthier foods, like tonight. I also like peanut-butter cups, and sometimes I even eat kale."

"Good for you. So, was it my father who introduced you to the junk-food world?"

"You might say that. I know he loved chocolate-chip cookies, brownies, and cupcakes…just about anything with chocolate in it or on it." Annie grinned. "So, to change the subject, did you enjoy the dinner we made?"

He laughed. "We? I don't think I can take credit for that."

"Yes, it was a joint effort. The carrots were great."

"Let me tell you, dinner was the best food I've had in a long time. The chicken was your recipe, and you're a terrific cook. I had no idea you had such a unique talent for cooking. I know you're a great nurse, and all our patients love you, but who knew this?"

"Thanks so much. I'm not used to cooking compliments. My neighbors like everything I make. Probably because it's free. Who doesn't like free food? It's great to have friends in the building; it makes the nights and weekend more enjoyable." She wanted to say less lonely, but she didn't. She didn't want to sound pathetic. "What about you? Friends in your condo?"

"Nope. Never had time to talk. But, since I've had Gracie, neighbors seem to be a lot friendlier. Or maybe I'm more approachable. Probably both."

"Could be. Dogs are a great icebreaker. So, now that you've heard my little junk-food secret, what about you? What do you like to eat?" She pretended otherwise, but there was very little about him she didn't already know.

"I'm a steak-and-potatoes kind of guy. I do have a sweet tooth every now and then. I love cheesecake with blueberries."

Annie laughed. "Guess what? I have some. I was planning on bringing it to the office, since Charlotte has a bit of a sweet tooth. Are you hungry for dessert? I know it's late, but what the hell?"

Noah smiled. "You bet. It's still snowing, so I can stick around for a while if you don't mind. It looks pretty bad out there."

As soon as Annie left for the kitchen, Gracie moved in. "You might want to kiss her again," she told him. "Girls like it when you show a sweet, affectionate side."

Noah shook his head. "I don't think so. I can't just kiss her again for no reason."

"A no-reason kiss is romantic."

"And you know that because you've been kissed for no reason?"

"Very funny. You have a reason; you like her. Isn't that enough? You already had one kiss."

"Maybe I shouldn't have."

"Man, you need help in this thing they call love."

"Not usually."

"Then why is she different?"

"Why don't you tell me?"

"Later. Annie can't see me talking to you. That's one of the rules."

"Rules? Whose rules?"

"Hey, do you tell me everything?"

"Of course not. I haven't known you long enough."

"Using the weather as an excuse — nice touch."

When Annie came back, she looked at Noah strangely. "Did I hear you talking to someone?"

He held up his phone. "Just the service. Seeing if anyone needs me. Force of habit."

Annie placed a slice of cheesecake on the coffee table. "I hope you like it."

"Looks like it came out of a magazine ad."

She watched as Noah slowly took a bite — first a tiny bite, then a little bigger, and then it was full speed ahead. Noah grinned. "This is incredible. You really made this?"

"I did, and I'm so glad you like it. I was trying out a new recipe last night. I had no idea I would be having a guest for dinner."

Noah seemed surprised at how well they were getting along in a social setting. They always had at work, but this was totally different, and Noah was really enjoying being there. He didn't want the evening to end, which was unusual for him. Usually, he was on the run once dinner ended.

"Annie, I think I need to tell you something." Annie figured it was time to go, as Noah paused to catch his breath. "This evening was great. It's wonderful that we have so much in common, and now with our dogs. I'm sorry it took so long."

"The evening has been nice, hasn't it? I loved going to meet your basketball friends. It was such a pleasant experience. I was so touched by your warmth toward the kids, and how much it meant to them to have you in their corner."

She watched as he looked at her in a very different way. His gaze was as soft as a caress, and left her whole body tingling. She was hoping for another kiss, but Noah seemed anxious.

Gracie was watching, and came away convinced that there was a sense of nervousness on both sides, which meant the opportunity for another kiss was going to pass quickly. She was disappointed, but confident it would happen again.

Once Gracie and Noah were in the elevator, Gracie couldn't help but add her opinion. "You know she really likes you. You had a perfect chance, and you blew it."

"I didn't. I just didn't want to push too much. We work together every day. I don't want to make it uncomfortable for us in the office. Let's just leave it for now."

"Fine," Gracie said with attitude, mumbling to herself. "The ball's in your court, for now."

Chapter Eight

From the moment Anne walked into the office, Charlotte had a hunch something was going on. Working together for years gave her some insight.

"You didn't answer your phone last night. So, I just assumed it was for a good reason. Was I right?"

"Yes and no. Well, my phone was off, but for a good reason."

"That sounds promising. Is the plot going to thicken?"

"Not in the way you think," Annie replied with a little grin.

"Just seeing how your adventure with Mr. Right went last night. Anything I should know about?"

"Actually, there is. Noah sponsors a team of spe-cial-ed kids. He's their coach. It was terrific watching him. He's great with kids here, but this was different. Kind of close and personal."

"Wow, why didn't he ever say anything to us?"

"You know how Noah keeps his little secrets. You know, the ones that we always end up finding out anyway."

"Apparently not this one," Charlotte said. "Not surprising, but terrific all the same. Where?"

"Midtown School."

"We have a few patients from there. How long has this been going on?"

"For a while, and the kids just love him."

"Noah really is a great guy."

Annie smiled. "We both already knew that."

"What a catch. If I were younger, oh boy…never mind. He's not my type, but he's yours." Charlotte gave a hearty laugh.

"I don't have a type."

"You do, but you don't know it. Noah's your match. You mark my words. He's the one for you."

"And if he's not? In your crystal ball, is there anyone else in the running?"

"Nope, because it's him. Noah Meyers is your destiny."

❤ ❤ ❤

Noah had to stop at the hospital before work. When he called in and said he would be late, Annie knew she had to start the ball rolling. She needed to get the patients ready so Noah could make up the time once he came in; otherwise, the entire day would be off. Annie knew from experience that if one kid started to cry, others would do the same. If they got bored enough, they'd mess up the rooms, and it would take more time than usual to clean up. Annie didn't feel like staying until nine that night.

"Charlotte, can you do me a favor today? You know how fast things get out of whack here."

"No kidding. One or two long conversations with worried mothers makes some of the kids go berserk."

"That's pediatrics, but then there's Noah. He gives every mother the attention they need, so time's never a factor; he doesn't even wear a watch."

"I already know you want me to get lunch."

"No, we can order pizza. But, if you would do me a favor, the blueberry cheesecake I made for the office is yours."

"In that case, whatever you want is a yes."

Annie smiled, realizing her cheesecake must be almost magical. Everyone loved it. "It's not *that* good," she said with a laugh. "You don't even know what I'm asking."

"Well, let's have it. What do you need, babe?"

Annie whispered in her ear. "I need you to go to Noah's and take out Gracie. He asked me to do it."

"Are you kidding me? Dogs don't like me."

"Just this once. Gracie likes you. Just be nice and smile."

"I guess it'll be okay. This is a one-time deal, though. Got it?"

Annie hugged Charlotte and tossed her the keys. "You're a lifesaver."

❤ ❤ ❤

As soon as Charlotte put the key in the door, she was greeted by Gracie. She bent down and petted the dog's head, pretending to be happy she was there. "Well, it's you and me, Miss Gracie."

"Yes, it is, Miss Charlotte," Gracie said, though she had been shocked to see her. "Now we have time to talk."

"Did you just say something to me, or have I finally gone mad?" Charlotte hadn't even gotten a chance to take off her coat yet.

"I did, and I'm so glad you're here. They said if I had a problem I should contact you, but I guess they did it for me."

"They?"

Gracie looked up. "I'm a Jewish angel just like you are; we just have different jobs. I help couples find their way to each other. That is, of course, if they are meant to be. I'm here to bring Noah Meyers and Annie Porter together. This is a tough one. They're good people; they just need a little help. Well, maybe more than just a little."

"You can say that again. I've tried to help, even though it's not really my area of expertise."

Gracie wondered what she meant, but didn't want to act like a newbie. Besides, she was a little taken aback by the ringing in her ears, thanks to Charlotte's hearty laugh.

"I've been here for a long while," Charlotte continued. "I marry men who have not been good husbands, and I get them into shape for their next life. A few of them were terrible, but they became pretty good husbands in their next life with my help."

"Doesn't sound ideal," Gracie said. "It's pretty hard, isn't it?"

"You bet your ass it is. Some of the guys came to me as mean as a hornet's nest. I make them livable, and then they die. After a short spell up in Heaven, they can come back down and start over with a new woman. Pretty challenging work, but someone's got to do it."

"Are they as good as new then?"

"Better. Never got one back."

"And now?" Gracie couldn't help but wonder.

"I'm on a short hiatus. Alone, but happy."

"Great," Gracie said. "Then maybe you can help me..."

Chapter Nine

Visiting her husband was always the first thing on Rosalyn's agenda when she came to visit, whether she was in Chicago for a day, a week, or a month. She knew Noah would be home soon, and he could entertain Vera and Essie until she got back. He wouldn't be that shocked to find his mother's two best friends waiting for her to get back from her usual trip to the cemetery.

There was something so entertaining to her about taking a Chicago taxi. The rides were usually fast and uneventful. The drivers would say hello, ask where she was going, and then continue listening to music or talking on the phone. It was almost as if they were bothered by the destination. *After all*, she thought, *who likes to visit cemeteries?*

The cab drove down the long, narrow road and pulled up to an overcrowded section of the cemetery. The area was called the Garden of Remembrance. Rosalyn could remember when it wasn't that crowded; now there were only a few spots left. "Damn," she mumbled. "This place is jammed."

The driver didn't hear her at first, but he jumped when she screamed out, "Stop. I need to get out now. Visiting my husband."

When she got out of the cab, she brought the portable chair and bottle of wine she had picked up on the way. She explained to the taxi driver that she wouldn't be long, and that he should come right back in thirty minutes. It was still cold, but she needed private time with Ben, even though the conversation was one-sided — much like their life in the later years.

Rosalyn walked toward her husband's stone, opened the chair, and sat down beside the grave. The ground was a little icy from the previous night's snow, but the chair steadied after a few wiggles. "Benjamin, my love, we need to talk."

She opened her tote, and took out two small, plastic cups, along with the wine. "You have to help me, Ben. Noah needs to find the right girl so he can settle down and have a life. Have a talk with God. He might remember us. We went to temple more often than just the high holidays. Tell him Noah had a bar mitzvah, and don't forget that you did, too. We have a lot of positives."

While she was talking, she poured two equal glasses. "So, you need to send someone to Noah, just like in the movies. Work your magic." Then she stood up and smiled. "Remember how we used to hope he would find someone to spend his life with? I've tried to find the right one. Guess it's not working. I thought I was on the right track, but nothing so far. Nada."

As she was just about to pack up and leave, she added some closing words. "I promised him I wouldn't fix him up anymore, but I lied. He knew I was lying, but you know how Noah is always respectful. He smiles, and then does whatever he wants. That hasn't changed."

She sat there for a few more minutes, reflecting on their life together. "There is one other thing, Benjamin. Make sure she isn't someone who might have a little indiscretion. Or a few, like you, my love. Yes, I knew. Just for the record, I had one or two myself, which I know you never even imagined. You probably never thought I was passionate enough, but I was — just not with you." Then she laughed. "But, I loved you anyway."

Rosalyn finished her visit by pouring the rest of the wine on the grave itself. "It's your favorite. Love you, Benjamin. SOS. Help me find a bride for Noah."

Just as she was wrapping up, a man she didn't know was walking over toward the grave. "Are you visiting someone?" she asked.

He smiled. "I am, but I didn't bring any wine. You seem to come prepared."

Rosalyn returned the smile. "That's me, always prepared."

"Joseph Samuels," he said, as he reached out his hand.

"Rosalyn." She didn't like to give too much away when talking to a stranger. "Do you come here often?"

"Every week. I miss her more all the time. She was a good woman. And you?"

"I don't live here anymore; I'm in Florida now. When I come in, I like to blame him for anything that goes wrong in my life. However, I do miss him.

We had a few little problems. Who doesn't? We had love; passion, not so much."

"It happens. I understand."

Rosalyn stopped herself from saying anything else; she had said too much already. She rarely got that personal with anyone, much less a stranger. Still, for some reason, Joseph didn't feel like one. "What about you? Kids?"

"We never had a child, but we had a very good life. She was a wonderful woman who brought joy to me when I didn't think it was possible."

Rosalyn continued packing her things.

"Any kids on your end?" he asked.

"I have a wonderful son, thank goodness," Rosalyn said, "but I might be trying too hard to make sure he's happy. I'm hoping he'll find someone to spend the rest of his life with. I shouldn't admit this, but I have a bad habit of trying to find the right girl for him. So far, it's been a disaster. There's one still out there, though. I just need to find her."

"You can't push love, even when you try. Romance in a life doesn't always happen, but when it does, it's perfect."

"I would like to be around to see him happy."

Joseph helped her fold the chair. "Do you need a ride back? My driver can take you wherever you need to go."

"No thanks. I need a few more minutes alone, if you don't mind."

"We can wait."

"It's okay. I have a ride coming."

Part of her wanted to take him up on the ride, but she didn't know him. What if he was a murderer? She reminded herself that visiting his dead wife didn't automatically mean he was a good man — although she was interested in a man who kept his wife's memory in his heart.

"No problem," Joseph said, as he shook her hand goodbye. "Good to meet you."

"Good to meet you, too. It's Rosalyn Meyers. My name, that is."

As Joseph walked back across the paved road toward his limo, he couldn't help but glance back. He was fascinated by Rosalyn's stamina. A chair and wine, how amusing. There was something about her that he really liked.

Rosalyn picked up a few stones, and placed them on the grave to show that she was there. It was a custom she always observed.

❤ ❤ ❤

By the time she got to Noah's apartment, Vera, Essie, and Noah were all at the dining-room table, talking up a storm. Noah was laughing, and seemed very relaxed.

"So, how's my favorite mother?" Noah said, as he got up to help her with her coat. "I got you a beef sandwich, fries, and green peppers on the side. Is that okay?"

"Excellent. From Frank's?"

"You got it. I know your favorites."

Gracie was sitting on the floor beside Noah. Rosalyn bent down. "And you are?"

"Meet Gracie," Noah answered quickly, hoping Gracie wasn't about to say something and blow her cover.

"She's so cute. Well, you finally got your wish. You've wanted a dog since you were a little boy."

"I did. And here she is."

Vera laughed. "She's so cute and smart. She seems like a person. Isn't it funny how some dogs look right at you, as if they're going to say something?"

Noah smiled. "Yes, that's funny." He glanced down at Gracie, who gave him a look.

"I think you've been watching too much TV," Rosalyn said. "Dogs don't talk in the real world."

"Mom, come on, sit down," Noah said. "The food's still warm."

Vera and Essie waved her over, both too busy joyfully eating to say much.

"I get it girls, you look preoccupied," Rosalyn said. "They don't make beef like this in Florida. Noah, thanks so much for keeping the girls company. Your father says hello."

Vera literally spit out what was in her mouth. "Rosalyn, have you gone crazy? Ben can't be talking to you. He's six feet under."

"Don't worry, Vera, I'm used to this," Noah replied. "She knows he's not coming back."

"I'm not sure I even want him back," Rosalyn said with a laugh. "Sorry, Noah. Just kidding."

Gracie was under the table, pulling at Noah's jeans.

"Whoops, ladies," Noah said as he got up. "I need to take Gracie for a walk. Be back in a few."

Gracie didn't say anything while they were in the elevator, because they were joined by a couple of people one floor down. Once they got out, and she was sure no one was around, that changed.

"Noah, your mother's kind of funny. I like her friends, and they're crazy about you."

"They never had kids, so I'm the closest thing they have. I love them, but when the three of them get together, you never know what will happen. My mother's the one who wants me to find a bride. Vera and Essie get that it's hard to just snap your fingers and have the right girl come around."

"Your mother's right, though. No one should be alone. Annie is perfect for you. She'd be such a cute bride."

"We had one little kiss. One kiss does not establish a long-term relationship."

"My point exactly. You need to give her a chance."

"Maybe she's not interested in me."

"Famous last words. You can see it in her eyes."

"Gracie, I live in the real world. You think life is like a soap opera."

"And you don't? Where do you think they get the stories?"

"I think you and my mother will absolutely drive me crazy, especially if…you're not going to let her know you talk, are you?"

"Don't know yet."

"What does that mean?"

"Okay, let's do this again, and look at my mouth this time. I. Don't. Know. Maybe."

"Very funny."

Chapter Ten

Noah got up a little earlier than usual on Saturday. He didn't have office hours, but he had scheduled an emergency board meeting at Midtown. The group had quite a lot of things to discuss, and Noah didn't want anyone to be in a rush to leave. The bare fact was they needed to raise a lot of money quickly, or all their hard work on behalf of the kids would be for nothing.

Gracie wasn't about to sleep through it all. "So, do you think it's going to happen today?"

"What are you asking?"

Gracie gave him a look. "I wasn't born yesterday. I know all about it."

"How is that possible?"

"I'm not a mind reader, but I was listening when you were on the phone last night."

"I thought you were sleeping."

"Just for future info, I'm always going to try to be up when you're around. I don't like to miss anything. I take naps during the day, after my soaps. It's exhausting listening to other people's problems. However, on occasion, I get insomnia."

"Didn't know dogs got insomnia."

"Just like how you didn't know dogs could talk."

"Yes, I guess so. You talk, and I listen. This whole picture is out of whack. I really hope I'm not going crazy."

"You're not. Believe me, I've seen crazy. Maybe a little overanxious, but that's better than crazy. Isn't it?"

"I never thought of myself as overanxious."

"Maybe you'd better think about it, Doc. It's a strong possibility."

"A possibility you might have something to do with."

"You could say that."

❤ ❤ ❤

Noah thought he was early, but a few of the other board members were there before him. Group discussions were not his favorite pastime; he knew he was always more effective one on one. The other board members didn't always see his vision, but they usually made the right decision if he could convince them.

That was his plan for this meeting. The banks he approached were making their final decisions on their yearly funding programs, and he wasn't sure Midtown would be on the list. He knew it was a lot to ask, but he was asking for the kids, and he hoped his presentation would make a difference.

Noah took a few deep breaths. *Damn*, he thought, *maybe Gracie is right*. Maybe he did get overanxious.

The rest of the board strolled in, each carrying coffee and their notes for the meeting. Nine members showed up — three women and six men — which was terrific turnout. Still, he could tell by the looks on their faces that they were going to be focused on how fast they could get out of there. Noah had one shot at keeping their attention, so he didn't want to waste any time. When they were all seated, he leapt right in.

"Good morning everyone. So glad you could all be here today. I appreciate you coming in on a weekend."

Noah knew all the board members very well; in fact, he took care of some of their children. He was still nervous, though, and wished Annie was there to help him. She always seemed to know just the right words to get her point across. He had never seen her lose patience with anyone; he couldn't say the same about himself.

He was surprised by how much he was thinking about Annie. He had never felt as if he needed anyone by his side, but things were changing. It felt as if someone had put a spell on him. Maybe he drank a potion, like in the fairytale books his mother read to him when he was little. Annie wasn't there, though, and he had to get this done himself. He tried to shake off the feeling and focus on his presentation.

"Okay, as you know, we have a small situation," he continued. "Well, to be honest, it's not very small. Before we talk about the money, I thought I would show you the video that my basketball team and I made to help us get funding. Hopefully, instead of just numbers on a page, this video will show exactly how good our programs are for the boys. They are now friends, which for most of them was something out of the question not long ago. They love this program; quite frankly, so do I."

Noah's video presentation began by introducing each of the boys, then showed footage of them from practice and games. "Okay, now watch when we are about to begin, particularly when the boys shake hands with the other team. Do you see the happiness on their faces, and the joy they feel at being part of a team?"

The board members watched in silence. Noah knew he had their attention. "Keep your eyes on the camaraderie they have. Not only did their school-work improve, but their behavior changed. You can see how much more focused they are."

The presentation was short and to the point. No one said anything when he finished, so he wasn't sure what they were thinking. But, before he could ask anyone what they thought, there was a knock on the door.

Noah wasn't expecting anyone, but he opened the door and a man walked in. No one in the room knew him, including Noah, but it was the same man Rosalyn had met at the cemetery.

"Are you in the right room, sir?" Noah asked. "This is a private board meeting."

"Yes, I know exactly where am I am." Joseph walked toward the head of the table and smiled.

"It has come to my attention that you're in need of some money — quite a bit, from what I understand — to keep everything status quo at the school. Am I right?"

"You are, and forgive me for not introducing myself. Noah Meyers."

"Dr. Meyers, I'm aware of your generosity and the time you spend with the boys. The Midtown School is a wonderful place. Keeping challenged pre-teens engaged in after-school activities is a feat, and I hear you do it well. Let me introduce myself. I'm Joseph Samuels, and I can help."

The principal, Dan Davis, entered. "I see you all have met Joseph."

Noah smiled. "We're getting there."

"Can I sit, gentlemen?" Dan asked.

Noah laughed. "It's your school, of course you can sit. Joseph, you too."

Dan took out a manila folder and opened it. "Some things are out of our control. We have a great staff, and no one wants to keep this school intact more than me, but we have this ridiculous order to vacate our school at the end of the year. They're tearing down this building and redeveloping the land. Multi-home dwellings and a brand-new park, which would be nice. I mean, the park would be nice, but not the houses. But they want all the land."

Noah was upset. "We can't let this happen. This is a terrific place. Some great kids have been educated here, and they went on to lead very productive lives."

One of the women stood up. "Well, now that we're all here except for Charlie, and he gave me his proxy vote, what can we do? I, for one, don't want this school to close."

Another board member turned to Joseph. "You said you can help. How?"

"I have quite a bit of money, and no family to leave it to," Joseph said. "I would like to make a difference. I'm the developer who bought this land. I had no idea how important this school was until I met with Dan. We had a few talks, then a long meeting, and voila! I'm here."

Noah was shocked. Dan rarely came to the meetings — in fact, he could only remember it happening twice — but he was very dedicated, and knew more than anyone how much kids got out of being at the school.

"Here are just a few thoughts I had. I think you might be happy to hear this property will be torn down when the new school is built." Joseph reached for a drawing pad, and began to map out his intentions. "Here's what the new building will look like. There will also be a couple of high-rise building for the kids to live in when they graduate, if their parents see fit. This is going to increase the number of kids the school can accept. Let me tell you, this project is going to be the highlight of my life. What about you, Noah?"

"I can't believe what I'm hearing. I'm thrilled."

This was the calmest meeting they'd ever had. Everyone was listening; no one was checking their phone or having side conversations. Joseph Samuels had their attention.

Finally, Dan broke the ice. "By the look on everyone's face, I'm thinking this sounds like a plan. Seems like we may have something very special happening here."

Noah smiled. "This is a pretty terrific idea, Joseph. I, for one, love it."

Joseph stood. "I think this will work. Are you with me?"

A unanimous show of hands ended the meeting. Joseph, Dan, and Noah stayed back and continued with some preliminary plans. Everyone seemed to be on the same page, and Noah was happier than he had been in a long time.

Noah could hardly wait to share the news with Annie, so he decided to surprise her. His mother, Vera, and Essie had plans, so they were busy. They were going shopping and to a play. Since Noah rarely had a free day, he picked up Gracie and headed over to Annie's.

❤ ❤ ❤

He called from the car, not wanting to assume she was free, and realizing just showing up wouldn't be right.

"Annie, it's me, Noah."

"Hi Noah. We've know each other for a long time. I think by now I know your voice."

"Fair enough. Anyway, I hope you don't have plans. I have some great news to share with you."

"Nope, just started thinking about what to make for dinner."

"Don't make anything. I'm bringing pizza. Be there soon. Oh, is it okay if Gracie comes?"

"Of course. I love pizza."

After she hung up, Annie took a look at herself in the mirror. "Oh, my hair! Shit. I should have washed it."

In less than five minutes, Annie rushed around her bedroom, picking out a pair of jeans and a sweater. She started to get dressed, but decided she wasn't looking great and had to make some sort of a change. There was only one solution. She ran into the bathroom, threw her change of clothes on the floor, got in the shower, and washed her hair.

She quickly threw her clothes back on — after all, how hard was it to put on a sweater and jeans? She then tousled her hair in a cute way, pinched her cheeks, put on some lip gloss, and she was ready to go. "Better," she said. Then she misted herself with perfume. "Now what? This is nuts."

She didn't have much time to worry about the evening, because the doorbell rang just as she finished giving herself the once over. She took a few small, deep breaths and answered.

"Smells good. And I'm hungry."

"Pizza," Noah said as he handed her the box. "Hope you like Lou Malnati's."

"I love it. Haven't had it for a long time. Thanks."

Noah followed Annie into the kitchen, as did Gracie and Molly. *We've got quite a little family going on here*, Gracie thought. *We're celebrating. Yeah, this is a possible connection!*

Annie didn't know what they were celebrating, but this was the first time she had ever seen Noah this happy. "It's great that you're so happy, but are you going to tell me why? Or just keep me in suspense?"

Noah took off his coat and threw it over her chair. "Do you remember when we talked about the school needing a miracle? Well, we damn near have one."

Annie motioned for Noah to move the story forward. "So, tell me more. I'm excited to hear the news."

"Well, we were having a board meeting at Midtown when this older guy came in. At first, I thought he was in the wrong room. He was dressed to perfection, and he carried himself with such confidence. He seemed to know all about Midtown and the crisis we were facing. Making a long story short, he bought the land — but, instead of tearing everything down and leaving us no place to go, he's going to build us a new school, and even housing for the kids and their families. All financed by him. He wants to do something important for the community."

"That's incredible." Annie was tearing up. "What a great idea. Who is he? He sounds special."

"I've never met him before, but I'm sure we'll be seeing a lot more of him. He's friendly with the principal. Dan's a great guy, too. He was even happier than me, which is hard to imagine."

"Wow, that's incredible news."

Noah gathered Annie in his arms, and held her tightly while she threw her arms around him. For a few brief seconds, nothing else mattered. Gracie was thrilled, but said nothing. The last thing they needed was a comment from the dog.

Annie smiled, thinking how lucky she was to have this great-looking, magnificent man holding her — not that she hadn't dreamt of this moment. Noah was so intrigued by how wonderful it felt to have her in his arms, and he certainly didn't want this feeling to leave. All in all, their hug was a tremendous break for Gracie's plan.

"Annie, my God, you smell terrific," Noah said.

"I do?" She was really surprised he noticed, but was delighted that he did.

Gracie was watching, wondering if Noah was going to take the next step. She didn't have to wonder too long, because, in a split second, each of them slid back out of the embrace. *Oh no*, Gracie thought, *the moment has come and gone. Elvis has left the building!*

Gracie was wrong. Noah waited a second or two before he said anything. Without thinking, he swept Annie into his muscular arms and kissed her gently. There they stood, confused and overwhelmed, but this time they had one long, remarkable kiss. The touch of his lips was a delicious sensation for her, and the kiss was surprisingly exciting for him. Their first kiss was now overshadowed, as this one led to another and another.

Gracie was thrilled to see the happiness on each of their faces. She was rooting for more. *Baby steps*, she thought.

Noah slid back, looked at Annie's smiling face, and grinned. "Do you like cheese and onion?"

"I do, and it smells fabulous."

Their moment was just beginning, and each of them was secretly hoping for more. Noah looked down at Gracie, who nodded in approval. He wanted to laugh, but didn't.

Chapter Eleven

Chicago weather was unpredictable, so when the temperature dipped way below freezing, the three Floridians — Vera, Essie, and Rosalyn — decided it was time to go back to where it was sunny and eighty-plus degrees. Noah drove them to the airport, thinking of what a great trip this had been. No fix-ups and no fights. A record-breaking, wonderful time together. Perfect at last.

After they said their heartfelt goodbyes, with many good wishes, Noah decided to go to the hospital to check on a couple of his patients. One was in for appendicitis, the other for a tonsillectomy. Noah wasn't a surgeon, but he liked to make sure everything went well and that the parents had no questions. He knew surgeons sometimes weren't great at small talk.

When he finally got to the office, he was more than a little late, but he knew Annie was always good at filling time and comforting some of the crankier mothers.

What he didn't expect was to walk into his office and find his mother sitting at his desk. "Mom, didn't I just take you to O'Hare?"

"You did, and that was really nice of you. You're such a great son. Vera and Essie couldn't stop talking about you; they're always talking about you. And they loved Annie. They can't understand why I haven't been pushing you to take her out, but I told them that was ridiculous. You have known her forever, and you're just friends."

"You're right about that. We were just friends and now..." Noah trailed off.

"Do you want to elaborate?"

"Nope, nothing more to say. Let's just move on and talk about why you aren't on the plane with your friends."

"Well, I probably should have mentioned this to you, but I met a man at the cemetery. He asked me out for dinner last week when you were working, and I went."

"Why didn't you tell me?"

Rosalyn didn't answer.

"Okay, let me get this straight. You met a strange man at the cemetery, and you went out with him because…"

"He seemed so nice."

"And was he?"

"Yes, and yesterday, when I went back to the cemetery to tell your father a few things before I left, he was also there. Talking to his dead wife."

"How convenient. So, you talked and said good-bye. Then you told him you're going back to Florida…don't tell me you invited him to Florida."

"I did, but he's in the middle of a big business deal and couldn't leave town. He asked if I could get dinner tonight. It's like it was meant to be."

"I know how you like spur-of-the-moment decisions."

"You know, dear, I'm not dead yet. I said no to his request at first, but when I was just about to board the plane, I changed my mind. What the hell? Why not go? So, I'm here."

"Okay. I understand. I guess."

"Good, then you won't be mad that I might be staying in Chicago for a little while."

"When you say a little while, do you mean a day, a month, a year, or forever?"

"Forever? No, that's not happening. I'd just like to spend some quality time with my son before I check out. Is that too much to ask? I could go at any time. And when opportunity knocks, no need to give it to someone else."

"What does that mean?"

"We can talk about that later. So, can I stay?"

"Of course. You can stay. You know I love seeing you, but tonight I have something very special to do. It's going to be a lot of fun. I've been wanting to tell you about it for a long time, but haven't. Why don't you come with me and see for yourself?"

"It's a date. Will I be surprised?"

"Yes, but it's not a woman."

"Okay, I'm in," she said, with a little disappointment in her voice. "You know I want the best for you. I'm your mother. I want to see you happy. Is that so wrong?"

Their conversation was interrupted by Annie. She quickly walked in and, without looking, asked, "Are you looking forward to tonight?" When she saw that Rosalyn was back, she thought, *Oh well, I blew it.* "Rosalyn, hi. I thought you and the girls left."

"Obviously." Then she laughed. "I love it when you call us 'the girls.' Makes me feel young."

Rosalyn was very curious about what Annie's question meant. *Hmm*, she thought, *maybe there is something going on between Annie and Noah…or he might be having a secret romance with someone else.*

"Sorry, Noah," Annie said. "Didn't mean to just barge in."

"It's fine, my mother's coming too. Oh, what about your other plans, Mom? Sorry."

"I can meet him later."

"Really? Okay. He?" Noah still felt a little weird about his mother dating. He knew she did, but preferred not to think about it.

"Noah, come on," Rosalyn said. "It's just dinner. Don't get that look of disapproval."

Annie smiled. "Sounds great, Rosalyn." She wanted to end that conversation, realizing it wasn't going to end well if it kept going. She knew Noah got a little uncomfortable whenever his mother's love life was discussed. "Noah, are you ready to start seeing patients? They're getting a little restless out there in the waiting room."

Noah smiled. "I can hear them. Maybe we should get a bigger screen for the kids. Movies will work. Funny ones. Yes, that could solve the problem. Annie, will you take care of it?"

"I'm on it."

Rosalyn watched as Noah and Annie left the room. Sometimes it was hard for her to believe so many years had passed. She remembered the days when Noah was a little boy watching his father at work. He liked coming to the office with Ben and, even at eleven, he knew he wanted to follow in his father's footsteps and become a doctor. Ben was thrilled.

After that, anything Noah did was always wonderful in Ben's eyes. In college, Noah had a habit of spending more money than he had, but Ben always bailed him out. They had a special bond. Plus, Noah's grades were always seamless.

Rosalyn stood up and wrapped her shoulder bag around her arm. "So, what time should I come back?"

"I'll be done about five, but I can pick you up at the apartment later, because I'm bringing Gracie with tonight."

Rosalyn laughed. "I guess now she's really a part of our family."

Annie smiled. "That she is."

"Okay, fine by me," Rosalyn said. "Call when you want us to come down. Gracie's such a cutie. We probably should have had a dog when you were growing up. I'm admitting I was wrong."

Noah didn't answer. He just smiled, surprised she acknowledged it. Now his biggest worry was hoping Gracie didn't start talking to his mother.

♥ ♥ ♥

Annie was already at Midtown when Noah, Rosalyn, and Gracie arrived. She was busy making sure the parents were comfortable, and it looked like she was doing a fantastic job. Noah knew Annie would come through with flying colors, as she always did. She was a great organizer. He was starting to realize how much he relied on her.

Just then, he had a frightening thought. *What if she quit? How would I manage the office?* Then he thought, *It's not about the office, is it?* This wasn't supposed to happen. He was very happy with his life the way it was. Or maybe he wasn't, and his mother was right. He wasn't ready to make that kind of commitment; a dog was enough for now.

As Noah went to meet with his team, and all the kids surrounded and hugged him, Rosalyn saw how happy her son looked. She noticed the parents watching were all smiles, just like Noah. *What a thrilling night for all of them*, she thought.

Rosalyn motioned for Annie to come closer. "This is such a surprise to me," she said. "Everyone seems to love him. I had no idea. I don't mean about everyone loving him, just that he was doing something like this."

"I had no idea either. I just recently found out. You know how private your son is. We usually only talk about the office and patients. Nothing more."

"Did Charlotte know? She usually knows everything that's going on."

"I just told her about it. She had no idea."

"Well, now I feel better. Nothing passes by her. Like Ben's issues. She knew long before I did."

"Ben's issues? What issues?"

"Nothing, dear. It doesn't matter now."

Their conversation was halted when Rosalyn saw her son motioning for her. He wanted her to meet his team, and she was delighted.

"Guys, meet my mother."

The youngest gave Rosalyn a great big hug. "Hi, Noah's mom. I'm Sam."

Rosalyn returned his hug. "Well, hello there, Sam. So nice to meet you." Noah beamed at his mother's sweet gesture of support.

She was always great with kids. Rosalyn thought she probably should have had a few more, but her pregnancy with Noah was so tough that her doctors advised her against it. Sometimes, she wished she would have adopted another, but the timing wasn't right, and then it was too late. One more mistake. She had far too much guilt stowed away in her mind about everything. *That Jewish guilt can kill you*, she thought, *if you live long enough to let it.*

Noah motioned for Sam to join the rest of the team, as the game was about to start. Rosalyn kissed her son's cheek. "Why didn't you tell me? This is wonderful."

"I don't know. I should have. That's why you can't always reach me. Now you know where I go after work. The cat is out of the bag, so to say."

"I just want to let you know that I think your father would be so proud of you. He would have loved this."

Noah was pleased. He was starting to get the feeling that it was time to stop second guessing everything he did. He didn't mean in his professional life; he knew he was a good doctor. His personal life had been another story, with his mother's fix-ups the closest thing he had to a booming social life. Now things were changing, with his team. And Gracie. And especially Annie.

He couldn't seem to shake off why he was constantly thinking of Annie. He had known her for years and always respected her, but he had never thought of kissing her, or going one step further and loving her. For that matter, he never thought about loving anyone enough to have a meaningful relationship. He was right; it was like a spell. If he wasn't so superstitious, he would allow himself to think about that.

While keeping his eyes on the court, Noah bent down and whispered to Gracie. "You're not going to talk to anyone else, are you?"

"Not sure what you mean, Doc."

"You're not going to tell me, are you?"

"Nope, go to your boys. They need you. Don't worry, Noah. I'll be quiet as a mouse. Stop worrying; you'll get an ulcer."

Noah gave Gracie a look. "Well, there's one thing you don't know about me. I already have an ulcer."

"Me too," Gracie replied with sincerity.

"Is that true?" Noah thought it was strange. Then again, everything about Gracie was strange.

"Nope. Just checking to see if you're really listening to me. Strong as a horse."

Noah laughed. "Okay, I get the message."

The buzzer sounded, and the game was about to begin. Noah picked up Gracie; he didn't want her roaming around. After all, she probably shouldn't be there, but most of the kids had asked Noah to bring her to the game.

"Can you put me down, if you don't mind?" Gracie whispered. "You're smothering me. Talk about your mother being possessive."

Noah stooped down and placed her beside him. "I'm glad to have you, even if you're a little too opinionated."

"I may have told you this before, but I love being with you."

"Good to know, but that doesn't mean I have to agree with you."

"Exactly," Gracie looked up. "Looks like I'm in."

"Who are you talking to?"

"I didn't say a word. Did you hear something?"

"No, guess not. My imagination."

"Must be."

When Rosalyn glanced over toward the door, she saw Joseph. He didn't notice her, but she couldn't help but smile. She wondered why he was there. *He really is a handsome guy*, she thought. *So well-groomed and confident.* His profile was rugged and strong. His thick, gray hair made him that much more attractive. Something unexpected was happening inside her, and she was excited by the possibilities.

Rosalyn was still watching the game when a young woman with a heavy coat and scarf sat beside her. "Mrs. Meyers?"

"Yes. That's me."

"I just wanted to tell you what a terrific son you have. My boy didn't have any friends, and he never smiled. But, since your son enrolled him in this school, he has changed into a happy kid. Thank you for raising such a wonderful young man. All the parents love Dr. Meyers."

"That's so nice to hear. My name is Rosalyn."

"Jackie, and my boy is Sam."

"Sam is a lucky little guy to have such a nice mother. This is such fun, isn't it?"

"It's been fabulous. I never thought my son could be this happy."

Both mothers sat there, watching the kids play. Rosalyn couldn't help but notice how closely Annie was watching Noah; in fact, she never took her eyes off him. Rosalyn liked that. Annie might be the one. She smiled and took a deep, satisfying breath.

The boys were making baskets, one after another. Noah's team was on fire, and came back to tie the score. By this time, Rosalyn was standing up and cheering. She was starting to feel young again. So many years had passed, but she still remembered going to all Noah's games and wrestling matches when he was a young teen. She hated those meets; she was always fearful he would get hurt. Nevertheless, she was always there, supporting him in everything he did.

She was also starting to wonder why she had never thought of Annie for Noah before. She'd been such a big help to Ben around the office, and then to Noah, and Rosalyn had always liked her. If she was truthful, it should have been so obvious. Now when she closed her eyes at night, instead of wondering who Noah could marry, she would think of Annie.

Annie was thrilled by how great the boys were playing. She stood up and whistled. "Go guys, go!"

"That's my son," Rosalyn shouted. "He's the coach."

Noah heard his mom and smiled. He whispered into Gracie's ear, "One up for me."

Now, it's time for him to find a wife, Gracie thought to herself. *No, cross that out; he's already found her. He just needs to open his eyes. She's right there, waiting in the wing.*

A few minutes into the game, Rosalyn turned to Annie. "How long have you been in love with him?"

"Who?" Annie asked, pretending she didn't understand.

"Annie, honey, you can't fool me. You know who I'm talking about. How long?"

"A long time. Do you think he knows that? Anyway, he's a confirmed bachelor."

Rosalyn laughed out loud. "Sorry, honey. I didn't mean to make fun of what you said. They're all confirmed bachelors. How can I help?"

"No thanks. I'm good."

"Well, then I'll have to stop fixing him up. I can't believe all the time I put into trying to find him the right girl, and then he found her standing in front of him." She hugged Annie. "Annie you're perfect. I think you know a lot more about him than I do. I'm hoping my son will see the light."

"I don't know. It may never happen."

"You two are meant to be."

"Roz, I love you like a mother, but I don't know. I'm not sure we'll ever be a we."

"Take it from me. You will. Do you believe in destiny?"

"Maybe."

"Even if you don't, I do."

Annie looked across the room, and smiled when she noticed someone eyeing Rosalyn. She tapped her on the shoulder. "Rosalyn, there's a man who's been staring at you the entire time we've been here. Do you know him?"

"Yes, as a matter of fact. I do."

"Really? Does Noah know about him?"

"Not much. There isn't much to know yet."

"Look, he's on his way over here."

Rosalyn smiled. "He's the man I'm having dinner with. He's pretty good looking, don't you think?"

"Very. How long have you known him?"

"Not long at all." Rosalyn held onto Annie's hand. "I met him at the cemetery."

"You're kidding?" Annie couldn't help but be amused.

"Nope. Who'd make that up?"

Annie gave Rosalyn a hug. "Good for you."

Annie had always loved Rosalyn. There were many days when she came to the office on her own, just to help out and give advice. She was wonderful to every one of the girls, and each of them saved their questions for when she visited. In fact, Rosalyn was the one who convinced Annie to go to nursing school. It turned out to be the best thing Annie had ever done, and Annie's loyalty to Rosalyn was eternal.

"So, is this why our dinner was postponed?" Joseph asked.

Rosalyn felt like a young girl when she looked at Joseph. Her knees were weak, and not because she was old. Even Ben never made her feel that way.

"Joseph, meet Annie."

"Hi, Annie."

Annie gave her usual sweet smile, which immediately made her approachable. For Joseph, though, it had another effect. Her smile instantly reminded him of someone he knew a long time ago. Francine Weller, his first real love. Their smiles were so similar that Joseph wondered if that was just a coincidence.

Annie felt Joseph staring at her, but let it pass. She didn't know him, but his reaction sure looked as if he recognized her from somewhere.

Rosalyn was a little concerned about Joseph; his face turned as white as a sheet. "Are you okay, Joseph? It looks like you just saw a ghost."

"I actually think I might have." He quickly changed the subject. "So, are you hungry? I saw you cheering like a real fan. Hopefully you worked up an appetite."

"This is I the first time I've met the boys. I had no idea my son was doing this, but I'm thrilled. Now I know why he's been so busy."

"Noah's your son?" Joseph asked in surprise. "Great guy. I admire what he's done here."

"Thank you. How do you know my son?"

"I just met him the other day. I know Midtown's principal, Dan, and he filled me in on the school's needs. I wanted to help the minute I heard about it. We've got some great plans for this place."

"That sounds wonderful, Joseph."

"You've got yourself quite a son."

"Thank you. I happen to agree." Rosalyn smiled, confident in her son's abilities. "I don't know all the facts, but I'm sure Noah will tell me about the plan. Not that I wouldn't like to know everything, but that's not how he rolls. He usually gets around to it."

Annie smiled. "Ditto for me. Noah's just a little bit secretive."

Rosalyn laughed. "Good way to put it, dear."

Annie added. "You know, Joseph, you're doing a wonderful thing. Noah was waiting for a miracle."

"When you have more than you need, it's time to give to others. That's what I intend to do. I'm pretty excited for this project to be underway."

Rosalyn admired what he said and, as sure as she was standing there, she hadn't expected to know anyone. She might have found herself another gem. *Funny*, she thought, *thinking that Ben was a gem*. Still, despite his problems, she knew he had been a good man.

Annie decided three was a crowd. "If you don't mind, it looks like Noah needs some relief with all the parents and kids circling him."

"Sure, bring him back with you," Joseph said.

"You got it," Annie said as she turned away.

Joseph's mind was in overdrive. He couldn't get Francine out of his mind. Not only did Annie look like her; some of her mannerisms were so close it was scary. Especially the way she turned away. It thought it couldn't be a coincidence.

He met Francine when he was a young man, while he was working in maintenance at a neighborhood drugstore. His future was up in the air, but he had ideas and a plan. He was going to be rich; he just didn't know when, or how.

It didn't seem like a perfect match. He was ordinary, and she was not. He was poor, and she was rich. He had no formal education, and she was educated. They had one important thing in common, though — he loved her, and she loved him.

The last time he had seen her was the most romantic night of his life. He had spent nearly his entire paycheck on their dinner. He had asked a friend if he could use his apartment, and he worked all day preparing dinner, which was his first try at cooking.

When Francine walked in, the lights were low and the candles were flickering. The house smelled of cinnamon from the apple pie he made for dessert.

Everything was perfect. There were red roses on the table and a small box with a red ribbon on the top. Inside was a ring with a very small diamond, but it was all he could afford. Francine was so excited that she cried. Immediately, she put the ring on, and smiled when it fit like a glove.

Joseph knew he would love her forever, but he had no idea that her parents would send her away the very next day. As soon as they realized the man she was in love with could not support her, they asked Francine to stop seeing him, but she hadn't listened.

So, they made alternate plans and shipped her to a school on the east coast, and Joseph never saw her again. They were certain she would be better off without him, but they were wrong. At least in his opinion.

He never got quite over her. Now he was certain that Annie looked exactly like Francine had, and that made him think about a love he rarely let himself remember.

He wondered how to find out about Annie's mother. He barely knew her, so how could he ask? If she was Francine's daughter, he was certain she would have known nothing about her mother's life before her. He would have been out of line asking, so he decided not to. He would do some research. He had a weird feeling in his gut that he was right.

Suddenly, Joseph's memories were interrupted by a pat on the back and a handshake. "Joseph, so glad you came," Noah said. "Isn't this a wonderful place?"

"Yes, and what you're doing is terrific. How about joining your mother and I for dinner?"

Noah was surprised, but tried his best not to show it. "That would be nice, but Annie and I promised the kids pizza." He looked over at his mother with a questioning smile.

Rosalyn knew what that grin meant. "Met him at the cemetery," she whispered. She could tell he was shocked to find out Joseph was the one she'd met.

"You two go ahead and have some fun," Noah said, then kissed her cheek.

Rosalyn smiled. "Noah, the kids did a wonderful job. I'm so proud of you for taking the time to join in."

Noah walked off the floor and into the locker room. He raised his arms in victory as soon as he saw his players' smiling faces. "What a night. I'm so proud of you guys. You were terrific on the court. Time for pizza."

Sam ran over to Noah and gave him a big hug. "We were good, right?"

"You were all great."

Chapter Twelve

That night at Noah's apartment, Gracie jumped on the bed, waiting for Noah to settle in before she brought up the subject of Annie.

"So, Noah, not only did the boys win, but you made your mother a very proud woman."

Noah laughed. "You've got that right. Finally, I landed on top. I know she loves me, but tonight I think I showed her a different side of me. I think she liked it."

"She did. So, when are you going to tell her no more fix-ups?"

"She promised tonight, but I don't think she'll stick to it. It's her lifelong mission to see me happily married."

"Well, if you to promise not to be mad, I can help you," Gracie said. She fidgeted on the bed, trying to get comfortable.

"How? Rosalyn Meyers is on a mission, and she won't stop until she gets me married off."

"I have a little test."

"You're kidding, right?"

Gracie looked at him. "Noah, do you, or do you not, want your mother off your back?"

"I want my mother to be happy, but of course I want her off my back."

"She's overanxious. A lot like you."

"She means well. Do you really think I'm like her?"

"I haven't known either of you long enough to make that determination, but possibly."

"Well, you'll see I'm nothing like her."

"If you say so. Now, let's get down to the matter at hand. Annie is very interested in you. I think she's in love with you."

"That can't be right. I'm sure she's just enjoying a closer relationship with me, as I am with her. It's been pretty nice, but I don't know that it's love."

"Let me put it this way. Are you in love with her?"

"I think she's great. Always have."

"You didn't answer my question. Do you think about Annie when you're not with her?"

"I suppose I do."

"Yes or no? Did you go to medical school?"

"Of course I did."

"And were you at the top of your class?"

"Yes."

Gracie was a little annoyed. "Okay, then, answer the questions to the best of your ability. We need to finish this. Do you care about what Annie thinks of you and the decisions you make?"

"Yes."

"Great, now we're getting somewhere. Do you admire her?"

"Yes."

"Can you live without her?"

"I don't know. Contrary to what you believe, I have a good life already. I, for one, don't constantly think about marriage."

"Well then, you need to take her away for a weekend, because you *should* be thinking of getting married."

"Oh, is that your assessment?"

"You know, you're not getting any younger. You need to get to know her in a different way."

"Like sex."

"Like romance."

"Not sure that's my style; I'm not good at romance. What if she says no?"

"Hey, if I know anything about women, she'll go, and you can figure it out. Thanks to your mother, you've already gone out with more than your share of women."

"True."

"If I got an invitation to go away with a handsome, smart, nice guy, you can bet your ass I'd pack my bags and be ready to go. It's all up to you, pal. Make it happen."

"It wasn't too long ago that I thought I was just a regular guy. Now I'm sitting here talking to a dog, who's giving me a love test, and I'm answering."

Gracie stared at him. "What's your point?"

Chapter Thirteen

For dinner, Joseph took Rosalyn to one of his favorite Italian restaurants. The staff knew him well, which made the evening very pleasant. The servers were constantly showering them with extras. Their water glasses were refreshed after a sip or two. Fresh bread was placed in the basket, so it would stay soft and deliciously warm while they were eating dinner.

Rosalyn couldn't help but be impressed. She didn't know much about Joseph yet, but she was seeing a man with a place in Chicago unlike that of anyone she had ever known. She used to think she couldn't be impressed at this stage in her life, but she was wrong.

Joseph made her feel special — wonderful and young. She wanted the night to go on forever, and couldn't wait to tell Vera and Essie about Joseph.

While the two of them were sharing a dessert, there was a short pause in their conversation. Finally, Rosalyn chimed in. "Joseph, can I call you Joey?"

He smiled, remembering that Francine had called him that. He nodded and gave her hand a little squeeze. "I would like that."

"Joey, this night has been so much fun. I feel as though we have known other for years. Besides that, I feel pretty damn young. I would like this evening to go on forever."

"Me too, Roz. It's okay to call you, Roz, isn't it?"

She smiled. "Of course. I'd like that. I always wanted Ben to call me Roz, but he liked Rosalyn better. So much for what I liked. Don't get me wrong. Ben was a good man, but a little over the top in the stubborn department."

"Seems like you knew him pretty well."

"Almost forty years of love, fights, and understanding. Looking back, it was good. Sometimes our minds have a way of forgetting. What didn't make us happy at one time now seems insignificant."

"That sounds as if you both got each other."

"I guess you could think of it that way. We had a good life. At the end of the day, most of it was worth remembering. Nothing in life is perfect. We can get close, and that should really be enough."

Joseph smiled, inspired by Rosalyn's way of thinking. He could have used that sentiment in his own life.

"Well, now that we've got that out of the way, I want to explain why I couldn't take my eye off Annie. I could feel you watching me."

"I did wonder about that."

"She reminded me of someone I knew very well, years ago. Especially her eyes."

"Were you in love with her?"

"I was, but we never married, and it was a long time ago. Anyway, enough about old loves and the past. We're in the future. I think it's so great to be with someone who enjoys the same things I do. There's something to be said about a woman who knows what she wants. If she likes dessert, well then, all the better."

"Well, that would be me. To a fault. Never been much for dieting."

"Don't know what you looked like before, but you're a beautiful woman. I'm very interested in you."

She blushed. "I'm not used to this much attention, but I've got to say it's pretty terrific."

"Maybe I shouldn't say this, but I'm really attracted to you. That doesn't happen often."

"Well, it's good to hear. I've been so busy trying to find the perfect match for Noah that I rarely think of myself as someone who should be going on dates."

"Isn't that what we're on?" Joseph laughed.

"Sometimes I find myself thinking I know what's right for him, but the truth is I probably don't."

"You're his mother. I'm sure he knows what you're trying to do is in his best interests."

"Maybe it's in *my* best interests. I want him to find someone to love."

"Maybe he already has. Did you see how Annie and Noah looked at each other?"

"So, you noticed Noah and Annie too?"

Joseph laughed. "I did. I don't know either of them very well, but it felt like there was a spark."

"It looks like there's a strong possibility. The two of them may well be exactly what the other needs."

"Let's focus on what we need." Joseph placed his hand on Rosalyn's. "Let's make tonight about us. A beautiful woman like you should be wined and dined. That, my dear, is exactly what I plan to do. If you'll let me."

Rosalyn sat back and took a deep breath. She had to admit she was a little scared, but she was flattered. After all, she thought, a woman of her age shouldn't be feeling what she was feeling. But that was before she met Joseph.

Joseph was also a little nervous. He was putting himself on the line. There he sat, a wealthy, successful man scared that he might end the evening with just a kiss, when he wanted much more. He was feeling something he hadn't thought possible in a long time. He was acting like a silly teenager. *Feels good*, he thought, *damn good*.

Rosalyn sat back and enjoyed her chocolate-cream pie. Joseph ordered extra whipped cream. *Ten more points for Joseph*, she thought. *And he was already over one hundred points*. He lifted his spoon and enjoyed the pie with her.

They both sat there looking at each other, knowing this was not just a dinner date. Neither of them envisioned the way the night had gone, but they were both fine knowing there would be much more ahead of them.

♥ ♥ ♥

Rosalyn tiptoed into the apartment, only to find Noah sitting up, half asleep.

"Nice of you to join us," he said. "Where have you been?"

"Out to dinner."

"It's after three in the morning."

Rosalyn sat down beside Noah. "Look, you know I love you. I might be a pain in the ass sometimes, but you don't have to worry about me."

"Really? What does that mean?"

"I'm a big girl. My job is to worry about you; you don't need to worry about me."

"Is that a law? If it is, I've never heard about it."

"Why don't you go back to bed, and we can talk about this in the morning? I'm tired."

"Oh, you're tired. I've been sitting here waiting for you for hours. No call, no text. This hasn't been a very good few hours."

"So sorry. I had no idea. I'll call next time."

Noah was aggravated, but being overtired trumped everything. "Okay. As long as you're safe at home, we can talk tomorrow."

Rosalyn kissed Noah's forehead. "I loved seeing you and the boys. I'm so proud of you. Midtown is lucky to have you."

On his way back to his room, Noah marveled at how his mother always had a way of changing the subject when she didn't want to talk about herself. He guessed where she was, and he thought he was okay with it, but realizing her night was a lot more than dinner made him curious. He didn't like to think of his mother with anyone other than his father. Then again, his father had been gone for years, and he knew there were probably a lot of things he didn't know about his mother.

"Oh, Noah, one more thing. Joseph and I are just friends. Not to worry." She lied, but that was all he needed to know for the time being.

"Easy for you to say," he mumbled to himself.

Chapter Fourteen

Charlotte was about to leave the office when she saw Annie sitting at her desk, tapping her pen to the beat of her music.

"I thought you left a while ago."

"Nope, just sitting here looking at this note." She handed it to Charlotte.

Dinner at seven, my place, it read. *Can't wait to hold you in my arms. Looking forward to tonight. Noah.*

"You're kidding. This is from Noah? Our boss, Noah Meyers? I didn't think he had it in him. Go Noah! It's so romantic."

"Exactly. It's so unlike him."

"What are you thinking? Rosalyn? Did she write this?"

"Who do you think? This isn't Noah."

"Are you going?"

"I don't have anything to wear. Besides, we've had a few kisses, but that was it. Maybe I'm not his type."

"The hell you're not. And, whoa, how did you never tell me about the kissing?" Charlotte glanced down at her watch. "Come on, you're coming with me. My friend has a great boutique. Let this be my treat. I've never had a daughter, so let's have some fun."

"I don't have much time. I need to feed Molly."

"Don't worry, I can do it. I'll drop you at Noah's, and then get over to your house and feed Molly. Everyone will be happy."

Charlotte drove, fast and furious. Annie was a little bit nervous, holding onto the door like it was going to fly open. "I can call and tell Noah I'll be late. No need to get in an accident."

❤ ❤ ❤

The car jolted when Charlotte stopped in front of her friend's store. "Here we are."

It was quite small, and there were no customers. Only the owner, Meredith Charles, was there.

"Sweetie, my friend has a very important dinner date," Charlotte said.

"Not a problem, Charlotte. Give me a minute."

It took her a little more than that, and Annie was getting anxious. "I thought it would only be a minute," she said.

"Who's counting?" Charlotte asked.

"I am," Annie said. "I hate to be late."

"Sit down, Annie. He'll wait. Believe me, it will be worth his while. Meredith works miracles. Not that you need one," she said as she opened a few of the drawers. "You could use some sexy underwear. I'm pretty sure your underwear isn't sexy."

Annie's face flushed. "Guess not."

"Just what I thought," she said as she handed over a beautiful black-lace bra and panties. "Look at these."

"I don't need it to be that sexy."

Charlotte stopped and looked at her. "Yes, we do! Now go put them on while I check out what Meredith has in mind."

Shortly, Charlotte came out with a couple of things. "Here you go." She held up a gold pant and black tee. "Very chic, don't you think?"

Annie shook her head.

Charlotte held up a black-leather pant and white, see-through top. "No, too sexy," Annie said.

"Maybe you're right," Charlotte said. She went in back and came out with a simple black dress.

Annie smiled. "That's me."

"Put it on while I get you some shoes. What size?"

"Seven," Annie called out. "Not too high."

"Seven coming up."

Annie had the dress on by the time she got back.

"Looking great, baby," Charlotte said.

Next, Charlotte brought out a black high boot and another shorter boot. Annie wasn't sure if any of this was right. "Charlotte, I don't know."

"Hold it, Cinderella. Check out these pumps. Valentino always works."

Annie slipped them on. "Okay, I hope I can walk in these."

"Hope you're not walking. You can take them off if they hurt."

"Charlotte, it's just dinner…"

Next, Meredith sat Annie down and brushed her hair, flipping it over with gel. "Adorable, my dear."

Annie took a look at herself. "I don't know."

Charlotte tossed open Annie's bag and pulled out a lipstick and gloss. "I would scream if you didn't have lipstick."

Meredith added the finishing touches. Lipstick, and a smudge of it on her cheeks. "Voila! You look beautiful. One last thing." She sprayed Annie with a sweet, sensual-smelling perfume from Paris. "Wonderful."

Annie smiled as she took one last look. "Thanks, ladies. I guess I needed that. Doesn't even look like me."

"Oh, but it does," Charlotte replied, feeling proud. "I wish you were my daughter."

Annie kissed her. "That's one of the nicest things you've ever said to me."

"Don't count on more. Love you. Have fun tonight."

Chapter Fifteen

By the time Annie got to Noah's, she panicked. She was so nervous she wanted to turn back, but she decided it was now or never. She took a few deep breaths, and into the elevator she went. She imagined getting stuck; that would take the edge off the night. Hopefully, by the time they found her, Noah would have gotten mad and gone to sleep, and that would be that.

Noah was waiting for her at the door, and had the sweetest smile when he invited her in. Something had happened to him. Every time he looked her way, his stomach felt weird. If he wasn't a doctor, he would be in the ER by now.

"Hey," he said. He immediately regretted how dull he thought he sounded.

"Hey," she said. She thought her hello was just as tiresome.

As he helped Annie off with her jacket, Noah couldn't help but be mesmerized by the smell. "Oh my God. Not only do you smell fantastic, you look gorgeous."

Annie began to feel a bit more relaxed. "Just something I had in my closet."

"I think you're beautiful and, if you haven't figured it out by now, I really like spending time with you. I'm so happy you could come for dinner."

"Did you write the note?"

"About the note. Let me explain."

Just as he was about to tell Annie the truth, the smoke alarm went off.

"It's the chicken."

They both hurried into the kitchen. Smoke was everywhere. Quickly, Noah grabbed a box of baking soda and threw it at the flames.

Annie slid her hands into the cooking mitts on the counter and pulled out the pan. They both started to cough, not realizing that the alarm had already alerted the fire department.

Minutes later, four brawny firemen showed up, ready to chop away. Luckily, Noah and Annie had done the right thing, and the fire had already dissipated.

"Sorry, guys," Noah said. "We put it out. Didn't think about the alarm it triggered."

One of the firemen proceeded toward the kitchen. "We'll check it out before we sign off on it. Are you okay?"

Annie still looked beautiful, but a little scorched. Her face had blackened marks, and her hair was a bit messy. Noah, who usually looked perfect, didn't. His hair was slightly singed, and his hands were charred. The good news was they were fine; the bad news was the dinner didn't make it.

Gracie had a bit of shock. She was sorry their romantic night was a little less romantic than she had imagined, but she would just try even harder to make this match work.

After the firemen left, Noah put his arms around Annie and looked at her in a way she had never imagined. "Annie, when you walked in tonight, you looked so beautiful. Even though this evening had a little bit of a bad start, it's going to get better. I promise you that."

Then he kissed her. His kiss was surprisingly gentle, but her lips were trembling. "Annie, I don't want you to do anything you don't want to do."

"I know that."

"Are you okay with this?"

"I don't know. Part of me says, 'Go for it.' The other half says, 'What's the rush?' I'm so afraid we will ruin what we have."

Noah knew exactly what Annie meant, because he felt the same way. He held her tightly and hugged her. "I think you're the best thing that ever happened to me. I don't know why we never thought to do this before."

"Me too," she added. "Noah, let's not go too fast. If this is going to be good, and we want it to last, we need to take a few steps back."

Noah smiled. "What do you say we have dinner?"

"Good idea. I'm starved."

"Chinese or Italian?"

Before they could order, there was a knock at the door. It was Rosalyn. "What the hell happened here?"

"We had a little fire. Well, it was all my fault; this could be why I order out or go to restaurants," Noah said. "I guess I should have taken the chicken out.

Or, maybe I should have taken more peeks inside, just to make sure everything was okay."

"My God, this was my idea," Rosalyn said. "A bad one, it looks like."

"Also, half the building was at my door watching me make a fool of myself," Noah added. "It was quite a commotion. Actually, I would have been a little concerned if it wasn't my apartment. No one likes a fire in the building. A bit scary, don't you think?"

"Noah, honey, I'm so sorry."

"I know you are. Anyway, why aren't you out on the town with Joseph? Where is he?"

"In the car. I'm here to apologize to both of you."

Noah was shocked. "You're kidding, right?"

"Nope. I've seen the light!"

"The Jewish light?"

"The romance light. What you two decide is what you two decide."

"Where did this come from?"

"Joey has made me understand I shouldn't keep pushing you."

"Well, that's good news."

Noah and Annie each gave her a look that said they weren't quite sure whether to believe her.

"You have my promise," Rosalyn said. "I won't push you to do anything you don't want to do."

Noah shook his head. "Is that really going to ring true forever?"

Rosalyn smiled. "Honey, forever is a long time. Let's just say for now, and leave it at that."

"Fine, sounds like a good plan."

"Call me tomorrow," Rosalyn whispered to her son before she left. "We should talk."

Gracie had been watching everything since the smoke alarm went off and interrupted her shows. *Well there's nothing more for me to do now*, she thought to herself, as she walked back into the bedroom and finished her soap opera. *Remarkable thing, this on-demand TV.*

When Rosalyn got back to the car, Joseph seemed very upset. He had tears in his eyes. "What's happened?" she asked him. "I was only gone a few minutes."

"Well, I just found out what I suspected is true."

"And that is?"

"I hired a private investigator to find out…"

"What are you talking about? You lost me."

"It's Annie. She's my daughter."

"Oh, my God."

"I had Charlotte get me a few strands of Annie's hair. I felt a little sneaky, but I knew in my heart after meeting her that she was Francine's daughter. Now I know she's also mine. Ninety-nine percent. Annie Porter is my daughter."

Rosalyn was shocked at this revelation. "What are you going to do?"

"I don't know. How do I tell her after all these years of not knowing about each other? 'Hi there, you don't know much about me — and I don't really know anything about you — but I'm your father. So please make room in your heart for me.'"

Rosalyn stroked Joseph's back. "So sorry about this. It's going to be fine."

"I'm feeling pretty damn lucky to have found her. I never expected to have a daughter. It's just so unreal."

"Annie is a lovely young woman. I've known her for years. She's going to be very happy to have such a wonderful man for a father. It will be quite a bombshell, but there's always been a loneliness about her. Once she gets used to the idea of having a father, she will be happy."

"But all those years. It seems like she had a pretty rough road. I could have been there to make it easier on her."

"Why would she blame you for something you didn't even know about?"

"Maybe I should have tried harder to find Francine."

"How were you supposed to know she was having your baby? I'm sure you did what you could. It was a long time ago."

"I'll bet Francine's parents knew. What a shame. They hated me so much that they denied their daughter a chance to be with the man she loved. Everything would have been different."

"Do you want me to talk to Annie?" Rosalyn asked with empathy.

"No, that might make it worse. She needs to hear it from me. I'll tell her as soon as I figure out what to say."

Rosalyn leaned toward Joseph and kissed his cheek. "I've met a lot of men in my time, but you are by far the nicest, most considerate man I've ever known. She's a lucky girl. You're a good man, and don't you forget that."

"Well, right now I'm not feeling that way. Can we cut the evening a little short? I need to think about how to make Annie feel comfortable."

Rosalyn smiled. "Of course you do."

"Roz, I am so thankful to have you in my life. You don't know how much I wanted a child."

"And now you have one. Sometimes a surprise like this can be life changing. I'm sure you will find the right words." This time, Rosalyn gave him a sweet kiss right on the lips.

He smiled as he looked at her. "I'm so lucky to have found you. I love everything about you."

Oh my God, she thought, *he used the "L word." Wow.*

"I love you, too. You're one of the best things that has happened to me in a long time."

"Here's a little secret," Joseph said. "I fell in love with you the minute I laid eyes on you."

"At the cemetery? I doubt many relationships have started there."

"Yes, right then and there. When I walked away, after you said you needed some alone time, I remember thinking Ben Meyers was one lucky son of a bitch."

"I've never really considered myself a lucky woman, but I now realize I am just that — the lucky woman you read about who finds love twice. I was waiting for a sign from God for Noah, but instead I now have my sign. It's you."

Joseph grasped her hand before she got out of the car. "Thank you so much for being you."

Rosalyn smiled back. "Good luck. I'm here for you if you need me."

Chapter Sixteen

As Noah was getting ready for work, Gracie saw an opportunity. "Listen, I've grown to like it here, but you need to come to your senses," she began. "You can pretend not to know what you want, but I know Annie is the one for you. Stop being such a fool and admit it. Anyway, what have you got against marriage?"

"Nothing. Why would you say that?"

"Because I've noticed that your face gets as pale as a ghost at even the mere mention of marriage."

"It does not."

"Follow me. I want you to take a good look at yourself."

Feeling like an idiot, Noah followed Gracie into the bathroom. He looked straight into the mirror.

"Now," Gracie continued, "say, 'I'm not afraid of marriage.'"

"Fine. I, Noah Meyers, am not afraid of marriage." Then he looked in the mirror. "Okay, you might be right. I'm a little pale."

"Maybe you should see a doctor."

Noah looked down toward Gracie. "Very funny. Maybe you're right."

"Okay, let's pretend I'm a psychiatrist. Are you in love with Annie Porter?"

"I like her, and I might be in love with her. I'm not sure I've ever been in love, so maybe I don't what it is."

"Okay, let's try this again. Are you in love with the woman who is the perfect match for you?"

"I might be. Probably, yes. I don't know when it happened, but it did. I think."

"And you call yourself a doctor?"

"Being in love and being a good doctor are not the same."

"Maybe so. Now that wasn't so hard, was it?"

"You seem to get me to say things you want to hear."

"Take it from me, Doc. Women are like that. You'd better get used to it. When are you going to tell her?"

"On our trip to New York. I've rented a beautiful suite at a bed and breakfast."

"And you didn't say anything?"

"I'm not sure she'll go."

"Of course she'll go."

"What makes you say that?"

"Let's just leave it like that. Trust me. She'll go. When is it?"

"In a couple of weeks."

"Well, I guess that's better than nothing. And my hat's off to you. You did it yourself."

Noah laughed. "You might want to remember something. Long before you, I had a life."

"And how's that going for you?"

On Sunday, Noah was at a meeting for the school, and Charlotte offered to take Gracie. The office was on the agenda — not Gracie's first choice, but Charlotte needed to get some work done without any patients around.

Annie had offered to help Charlotte, so she met them there. She didn't particularly like paperwork, but Charlotte was fun to be around, and Annie didn't have much to do.

"So, Annie, how's it going?" Charlotte asked. "Progress or no progress?"

"I don't know. It seems like one step forward, one step back."

"I've noticed Rosalyn has stopped fixing Noah up. Is that because of you, or because she's too busy with Joseph?"

Annie laughed. "It still seems funny to see Rosalyn with Joseph. Or, for that matter, anyone other than Ben. I'm sure there have been other men, but what she did in Florida stayed in Florida."

"You know, Annie, she's human. Not just Noah's mother. Maybe she missed the pleasure you get from good sex. Now, she has her own private love machine. For an older guy, Joseph is kind of sexy."

Annie gave her a look. "You're kidding me, right?"

"Nope, he's kinda cute."

"Don't tell me you're interested in him, too."

"Nope, he's too good. I like bad boys. Always have, always will. Now, back to Noah. You should stick to it. He's a good catch."

"It's not like fishing," Annie said, surprised at her own analogy.

"Really, how do you figure that? You throw some bait, and then some more. If someone hooks on, you've got to work to keep pulling them in. If you're not strong enough, you'll fall into the water and drown. If you're strong, you'll pull that sucker in and make him see the light."

Annie couldn't help but laugh, and Gracie wanted to join the fun. To keep from laughing, Gracie closed her eyes. She put herself in serious mode.

"Maybe Noah has a secret life no one knows about," Annie said. "For all we know, he might have a few lovers."

Charlotte shook her head. "No way. Girl, you've got to think with confidence. He's yours if you want him. Just go out and get him."

Gracie was listening, but she really didn't know how much longer she could pretend to be uninterested. She knew that if she couldn't complete this assignment, her days on Earth would soon be gone.

It would be back to Heaven, or maybe worse. It was time. She had a voice, and she was going to use it.

"Ladies, please," she interrupted. "My future's at stake."

Annie stood there for a moment. She couldn't believe what she had just heard. "Gracie, did you just talk? You don't talk. Dogs don't talk."

"They sure do. Depends where they came from. I'm here for a while, and I wasn't planning to let you hear me, but this is a crucial moment. My job is in serious jeopardy, so what have I got to lose? Just so you know, Noah doesn't have another girlfriend. Let me ask you this. Have you noticed the way he looks at you?"

Annie wasn't sure about any of this. "Charlotte, is this really happening? Come on, this can't be true. Can it?"

"Yes, it's happening right now, despite orders from above," Charlotte said. "Gracie talks. She's here to help, but she was not supposed to let you know that."

"Sorry, Charlotte," Gracie confessed. "I had to."

"Gracie, my love, I understand. But you might be having a problem soon. Anyway, let's see how all of this goes."

Annie was bewildered by this whole conversation. "Charlotte, you know about this?"

She responded with a nod. "That's a subject for another time or place. Or not at all."

"I think I'm going to leave. This is too crazy for me." Annie was nearly out the door when Charlotte repeated the question.

"Annie, have you noticed the way Noah looks at you? Please answer."

"He doesn't look at me any differently than he looks at his patients, or anyone else," Annie said. "Noah's the kind of guy who looks you in the eye, and that goes for everyone he talks to."

Gracie gave Annie a look of doubt. "Annie, listen please. He absolutely looks at you in a unique way — and you look at him the same way. You're perfect for each other. It seems to me you both come alive when you're together."

Annie left like a bat out of hell. She was so confused and upset she didn't think the day could get worse. It did.

After a long, hot shower, Annie made herself some macaroni and cheese — her favorite comfort food. When that didn't help, she turned on a Hallmark movie. If she was going to be sad, at least she would have a reason. She hated to admit it, but the romance in those movies always gave her hope, like there was someone out there waiting for her. If it wasn't going to be Noah, maybe there was someone somewhere.

When she first heard a knock at the door, she wasn't going to open it, but she figured it was Wes wanting something to eat. The two of them had shared many quarts of ice cream to soothe the bad days; he had a lot more of them than she did. Until her recent dates with Noah, Annie had never been one for after-work socializing, so she was alone most of the time.

She was surprised to see Joseph when she opened the door. "Hi. I thought you were my neighbor looking for some food."

"Are you a good cook?"

"Well, I do love cooking. Some say I'm good at it. So far, no complaints."

He smiled. "Sorry. I don't like to come over on the spur of the moment, but I needed talk to you and it can't wait."

"Is everything okay? Rosalyn? Is she alright? Did something happen?"

"She's fine. Can I come in?"

"Oh sure, excuse my rudeness."

"Going somewhere?" Joseph glanced over toward a half-opened suitcase.

"Maybe. Noah wanted to take me to New York. There's a conference and he thought I might enjoy getting away. I'm still undecided."

"That sounds like a great idea. It's always nice to get away, even if it's just for a few days."

She smiled. "Maybe."

Annie had liked Joseph from the moment they met. He was so kind and attentive to Rosalyn, which was a definite plus in her world. If he made Rosalyn happy, that was good enough for her. Annie knew how deeply Rosalyn missed Ben, even if she pretended not to.

After Ben, Rosalyn seemed displaced every time Annie saw her. Even if she didn't let on that she was lonely, Annie knew all Rosalyn's jokes about Ben and their problems were just silly remarks that meant nothing. Ben and Rosalyn were a team.

Annie saw such a difference in Rosalyn when she was with Joseph. So did Noah; they used to laugh about it. Noah, of course, was happy not to have his mother's horrible fix-ups anymore. He thanked Joseph for making his mother see the light.

"Anyway, I hope we'll have fun on the trip," Annie said. "I've lived in Chicago all my life, and have never been anywhere. Never found the time."

"Well, it's good that you're going to be able to have some fun now."

"Enough about me. You came here for a reason. What can I do for you?"

Joseph couldn't quite get the words out yet. He had never had trouble talking to anyone before, but he was thinking about how Annie's life — and his own — would have been different had he known he had a daughter. That made Joseph feel worse, if that was possible, about the years he would have to make up. He knew the possibility of never gaining her affection was greater than that of her just saying, "Yes, that sounds wonderful. Let's start from now, Dad."

Francine should have told him. He had spent the better part of his adult life loving a woman who kept him away from his daughter. At times, his marriage suffered because he never got over losing Francine. No matter how he tried, she was always with him.

His love for her diminished in a flash when he found out she didn't think it was important enough to tell him he had a child. Now he wondered how he had ever loved her at all.

"Annie, I think you should sit down."

"Whoa, that bad?"

"After I tell you, you'll tell me if it's good or bad news. I think it's the best news I've ever had."

Annie sat, ready to listen. She had no idea how her life was about to change.

"When I was a very young man, I fell in love with a beautiful woman. I would have given her the world, but her parents didn't have anywhere near as much confidence in me as I had. They didn't think I would amount to anything, and they wanted their daughter to stop seeing me. If I were them, I might have reacted the same way."

"Guess they were wrong," Annie said.

"Even though I had almost no money, I scraped together whatever I had and bought her a ring. It wasn't very big, but she didn't care. We were in love. I asked her to marry me, and she said yes. The next day, I went to pick her up for dinner, but she was gone. She didn't mention anything about going out of town, so I was certain her parents made that decision."

Annie had no idea where the conversation was going. She didn't know Joseph very well, but it seemed painful for him to get the words out.

"Her mother said she would call me when she came back. I was young and naïve, and I believed her. It was just temporary, I thought. All of it was a lie. I had no idea she was never coming back."

"Did she at least call you, or send you a letter? Anything?"

"No, nothing. Not one word. I tried everything I knew to find her, but my resources were limited. It takes money to get to the bottom of things."

"I'm so sorry, Joseph."

"I was devastated. I couldn't eat or sleep. I was a broken man. I loved her so much I didn't want to go on living. But, after months and months of living without her, I tried my best to go on. As you can see, I made a life for myself, despite the devastating truth."

"A very impressive life at that." Annie smiled, and Joseph again saw Francine in her. It was painful telling the story, but it suddenly began to feel like a weight was lifted.

"I married a wonderful woman," he continued. "Ellie was her name. We had a great life, but the one thing I wanted was a child. We tried, but we weren't able. After years of being childless, we finally adopted a beautiful baby boy. He was so adorable, and we loved him to pieces, but he got sick. There was nothing we could do to save him. He didn't make it."

Tears began to fall from Annie's eyes. "I'm so sorry."

As Joseph continued, he felt that his heart was guiding him to come up with the right words. Even though his daughter was sitting right there, the disappointment of the past flashed before him. He was about to change his mind and walk out. Maybe he shouldn't just spring this on Annie, but it was too late. He was there, and she was listening.

"We were both so distraught. I put my heart and soul into making money, and I made plenty of it. You already know all about that. What you don't know is what I have just learned."

Annie shrugged her shoulders a bit. "What's that?"

"Well, when I met you, I immediately noticed that you looked like Francine. I thought it was my imagination. No one could be that beautiful, with such amazing eyes and a charming smile. Seeing you brought back all my memories and feelings."

"I remember wondering why you were staring at me when we first met. That's okay. I get it. I looked like her, and it triggered a memory for you."

"So sorry about that. One of the things money can buy you is the luxury of finding out what you need when you need it. Sometimes it might take a little time, but it does happen.

After we met, I hired a private investigator to get to the bottom of what I imagined could possibly be the truth, that Francine was your mother. I found out more than that. Francine was pregnant with my child when she left, and she had a daughter. That daughter is you."

Annie didn't say a word. She heard him, but the words began to scramble in her head. Nothing seemed real anymore. Her very identity was now a question. She could never have imagined this.

"Annie, please say something."

She began to cry. As Joseph inched closer, she pushed him away.

"I know this is a lot to take in, but all of it is true," he continued. "I'm your father." He handed

Annie a copy of her birth certificate. She refused to look at it. "Here are the adoption papers."

"I don't understand."

"Your parents who died were your adoptive parents. Unfortunately, Francine and her husband were in a car crash and died years earlier, so there was no other family to be found."

Annie felt as if someone had just punched her in the stomach. She couldn't breathe, thinking her whole life was a lie. Everything in her mind was upside down. Annie glanced at the documents. She read the words, but everything was a blur. *Mother: Francine Weller. Father: Joseph Samuels.*

"It was startling to see for me too," Joseph said. "I guess when she had you, she still loved me, because she didn't put 'unknown' or anyone else's name."

Joseph handed her a picture of Francine. As Annie looked at it, she couldn't help but see herself. Annie touched her mother's face, and the tears began to stream down her cheek.

"What if she just said you were, and maybe you're really not?"

"I had a paternity test done."

"Without my knowledge."

"Kind of. I had Charlotte get a few locks of hair."

"That explains my hairbrush disappearing."

"Annie, I'm so sorry. I know this will take some time for you to get used to," Joseph added. "I loved your mother, and I would have loved you with all my heart had I known. I'm so sorry."

Annie didn't know what to say. She was numb.

"I would like the chance to make it up to you."

"How does one do that?" Annie said as she stood up and opened her front door, motioning for Joseph to leave. "I think you should go."

"Can't we talk about this?" Joseph was beside himself. He expected her to be shocked, but this was not how he imagined it would be. *I didn't pass the test*, he thought. *Will I ever get another chance?* That decision would remain Annie's. The way things were going, Joseph suspected that it might never happen. She couldn't even look at him.

Right after Joseph left, Annie grabbed her keys and headed to Wesley's apartment. He was constantly asking her for advice — not that she was well versed in love — but now she was the one who needed a friend. She couldn't remember being this upset.

Annie had thought that not having a family made her immune to family squabbles, but she suddenly realized she was wrong. Knowing she had a father really complicated her lonely life. It especially got to her because, for years, she had prayed for a family.

When she knocked, Wes didn't answer, so she decided to wait until he got back. She sat on the floor outside the door crying, glad no one from any of the other apartments walked by. She was hoping Wes would turn up soon, and wasn't having an over-nighter with one of his friends. He had an occasional habit of disappearing for days at a time. Her rather uncomplicated life had become complicated, and she was very sad.

It wasn't that long before the door opened, and there was Wes. "What the hell are you doing on the floor — and crying, no less? So not like you, and so like me."

Wes lent her a hand and pulled her up. "Come on, tell me what's happened. I've got a date tonight, but it looks like he may have to wait. First things first. You're my family."

"Thanks. You're the greatest friend ever. I got some life-changing news today."

"Whoa, that sounds serious. Come on, I'll make you some coffee. Or does this occasion call for something a little stronger? Like whiskey?"

"No, coffee's good. Make it strong, please."

"Well, I need some whiskey."

After four cups of coffee, three cookies, and two pieces of the cheesecake she had made for his birthday, Annie finally told Wes what happened.

He didn't say a word until she was finished, which was not his style. He wanted to make her feel better, so he started his usual joking around.

"So, don't you think having a rich father's a good thing? I'll take him if you don't want him. Maybe he'd like a gay son. There's something to reflect on."

Annie forced a smile. "Thanks, but your charm isn't working that much."

"Is it working at all?"

"A little."

"Good. Then my job is done."

When the whole story was out, and she was a bit more composed, Annie had a few regrets. "I wasn't very nice to him. After he poured his heart out, I didn't have anything to say."

"You were probably in shock. I'm sure he knew that." Words of wisdom from Wes. He was trying his best.

"He's a really good guy. While he was telling me the story, I felt sorry for him. When we got to the part about me being his daughter, though, I just couldn't wait for him to leave. I missed having a father in my life, but now...I don't know what to say. It might be too late."

"No, it's not. Give him a chance. He didn't know. From what you're telling me, he's also very upset about being lied to. He's gone his whole life without knowing he had a daughter. If you look at it that way, you are both casualties of a lie. There's always someone who gets hurt. In this case, it's both of you."

Annie tossed the picture of Francine over to Wes.

"Oh boy," he said. "You are your mother's daughter. Look at the eyes and the nose. Oh my God."

"I don't know what to think. Now the woman I thought was my mother wasn't. She adopted me. This is terrible."

"Did you love her?" Wes asked.

"Of course I did. I had no reason to believe she wasn't my real mother."

"That's because she was. Remember what she meant to you, and just leave it at that."

Annie was shocked at the good advice Wesley was giving her. "Look at you, Dr. Phil."

She couldn't help but laugh. She was probably the only one she knew, besides Noah, who didn't watch the show. They always joked about that. Patients would come in quoting some of the things Dr. Phil said. The power of TV.

Her phone kept ringing, but she didn't answer.

"Before you do anything else," Wes said, "you should answer your phone."

She glanced at her missed calls. Five from Noah, and a few from Rosalyn. From the messages they left, she knew Joseph had filled them in. She wasn't upset that Rosalyn and Noah knew; in fact, she was fine with it, because she wouldn't have to tell them the news.

Annie knew this was something she couldn't just sweep under the carpet and pretend didn't happen. After years of praying for one, she had a father, but she was also deeply disturbed by the intrusion. Her private world was now open to discussion, and she didn't like that at all.

"Annie, you need to talk to Noah."

"Right now, the only one I need to talk to is Molly."

"Hey, what about me?"

"Sorry, hon. You know I love you, but Molly's my rock. A dog can be the greatest confidant you have. She's mine. I wish I could pick her up from daycare, but they're closed. I guess I lost track of time."

"I'll get her for you tomorrow. I promise it'll be okay, no worries," Wesley added.

"I can get her. I'm not going to work. Can't. I need time to think."

Wes didn't say another word. He was worried. For Annie, work was everything. Unless she had a fever and could barely move, she always showed up for work. She never wanted to let Noah down. She now came to the realization that a moment in time could change everything.

Chapter Seventeen

Annie decided not to go away to New York with Noah. Not only that, but she decided not to go to work the next day, or for many days after that. She did a lot of watching TV and cooking, anything to feel better.

She took long walks with Molly, and stopped at Starbucks for hot chocolate, but there was no cure for what bothered her. She felt betrayed by a man who called himself her father just because his name was on her birth certificate. A good man, but one she barely knew.

As for Noah, for the first time since he took over his father's practice, he felt disorganized and sad. He missed Annie so much he could barely get through the day. It was like others had said; he didn't know how much he'd miss her until she wasn't there.

Noah's life had suddenly become a lot more complicated. He didn't usually do well with unexpected events, but he wasn't going to let what had happened with Annie impact his patients' needs. His days were a lot longer and quieter.

After he made the rounds at the hospital and finished his office hours, he went straight home. He usually picked up dinner and went right to bed. Gracie was quiet, and usually fell asleep right after he did.

Rosalyn spent a lot of nights with Joseph, but she would call Noah in the morning just to say hi. It was so unlike her, but she knew when to back off. He appreciated that. The last thing he needed was a fix-up, because every day without Annie was surprisingly ordinary.

Noah attended several meetings that Joseph scheduled with the board, though Joseph sent his assistant to handle most of the questions and additions. He also knew when to stay away, but that wasn't what Annie would have wanted.

She never expected her problems to cause delays on the new project for Midtown. Construction had already started and, if the weather cooperated, everything was on schedule. Noah had to focus, so he did — but he also did it for Annie. He hoped she would return soon.

The discovery that Joseph was Annie's father was a big deal for everyone. There didn't seem to be a right or wrong. Everyone needed to take one step back and let Annie breathe. Joseph tried not to think about Annie, but found that impossible.

Charlotte picked up Gracie and brought her to the office on some days; on others, she went to Noah's apartment and fed her. After several days, Gracie and Charlotte were finally alone in the office. That's when the questions began.

"Charlotte, you're my go-to, so tell me — do you think I'll have to go back? I'm so happy with Noah and my life here. Maybe Annie wasn't Noah's destiny. What if there is someone else in the picture?"

Charlotte looked at Gracie. "It doesn't work like that. Sometimes it doesn't run smoothly. You must see it through. No one said this an easy job. Love is complicated."

"I thought if I do my job, everything would work out exactly according to the plan."

"Gracie, my dear, it's not like that. Think about it. Sometimes it takes an army to make it work. It's about the magic of love, and getting two people who really love each other together."

"Isn't it possible they're not right for each other?"

Charlotte laughed. "You haven't finished your assignment. If things don't go as planned, you need to figure out a way to make it happen."

"Really?"

"My dear, we're not magicians. We're angels with jobs. We just need to think about getting the job done. No one likes a lazy angel. It takes time, and you can't always fix things fast."

"Do I have time?"

"You have as long as you need, but you can't just do nothing. You haven't known the players long enough, but you need to rationalize every move and see it through, watching what they do. Then you have to make it work. Their decisions and actions are your pathway to your future.

"Look at it like we're heart surgeons. When a doctor is in the operating room, it's his or her job to do all the right things for a successful result. They don't walk away and say, 'The hell with it.' They fix it."

"Okay, Charlotte, you're the one with experience. I'm going to make it work. I like them both. I just need to know them better."

"No substitute for the real thing." Charlotte smiled. "There were times when I thought I wasn't going to be good at my job, but they gave me the go ahead to do what I thought was right. They want success up there. I'm so glad they let me stay and try new things."

"I hope I get lucky too," Gracie added.

"It's not just being lucky. You must put in the time to make love happen. You have the players; now you need the story. Just try your best, and you'll see something will come to you."

Gracie crossed her paws. "From your mouth to God's ears."

Charlotte laughed. "Don't worry, my dear, they're watching. They'll inject some help when they think you need it, but you won't know when."

Gracie didn't say another word. She was going off to meditate while Charlotte finished her work. Gracie had heard that meditating could help unwind even the most uptight of people — or dogs, she hoped. She wished she'd watched one of the yoga shows on TV and paid close attention to how it was done. Instead, she tried a few breathing exercises from memory.

Gracie exhaled through her mouth. *Not easy*, she thought, *but certainly effective.* She felt a little calmer. Then she closed her mouth and inhaled. One, two, three, four, breathe out. Good, done. Then she held her breath, counting to seven. She was afraid she would pass out, but she didn't. She exhaled, and there it was. She made a *whoosh* sound and counted to eight, again and again, until she was ready to go. *Got it!* she thought. *I'm freakin' renewed!*

❤ ❤ ❤

That night, it was just Gracie and Noah. Noah was very quiet. While he was reading some notes he took at the conference, he occasionally glanced down and saw Gracie staring at him.

"Trust me, I'm not going to die of loneliness. I miss her, but it's obvious she doesn't care too much about me, or she wouldn't have just left town without a word."

"Not true," Gracie said. "She left because she had too much on her plate, and she didn't want to address all of it. You know how she is."

Noah gave Gracie a look. "No, I really don't know how she is. And that's my fault. It's all on me, but I can't tell her anything if she's not here."

By the time Noah finished blaming himself, he was exhausted. He was in the middle of a sentence when his eyes closed and he fell sound asleep.

Gracie was happy. *It's about time*, she thought. *Poor guy; he's in love and he doesn't even know how it happened.*

Just as Gracie grabbed a blanket with her teeth and pulled it over Noah, she was interrupted by a knock at the door.

"Noah, honey, are you up? It's me, Mom." Rosalyn peeked in. When she realized Noah was sleeping, she closed the door, but not before Gracie pranced out. Rosalyn smiled, and Gracie knew it was time.

Just as Rosalyn was about to go into her room, Gracie asked her a question that certainly changed everything. "It's so great that you decided to stay in Chicago; I need a little help. Can I count on you?"

Rosalyn quickly sat down on the bed. She grabbed a magazine from the nightstand and fanned herself. "I knew it. My time has come. I'm hearing a dog talk. Help me, Ben! Help me!"

Gracie jumped on the bed. "Rosalyn, you're not crazy. You heard me talk because I do. I need to talk for my job."

"Oh no, this can't be happening."

"Rosalyn, it's okay. Just follow me. Breathe through your nose, and then let it out."

Rosalyn's eyes expressed disbelief. "Am I dead? I think I'm dead. I knew it."

You're not dead. You're just going to breathe again, and then we can talk."

Rosalyn took another deep breath, then another, and finally relaxed.

"Maybe I should explain." Gracie hoped she could reassure Rosalyn enough to make this whole mess blissful.

Rosalyn didn't say a word; she just listened.

"I need some help, and you'll agree once I explain why I'm here. I talk, but not everyone can hear me. I wasn't sure about you, but I think we can help each other, especially since you made a request through Ben."

Rosalyn's first instinct was to pull the covers over her head and sleep. After thinking about what

Gracie said, she immediately wondered about a few things. "Gracie, how did you know about Ben?"

"Since he died, didn't you keep asking him for a sign that he hears you? Someone sure did. This is going to happen. We're going to make it work."

"If you know about my request, tell me what you know."

"We have a common goal. You want Noah married, and I came down to help. We need to get Noah and Annie together, but nothing has worked so far. Now there's a complication, and we have our work cut out for us."

"Is Joseph real?"

"I'm sure of that. He must know someone up there, though, because his request was done one, two, three. He didn't need me, or anyone else."

Rosalyn still had questions. "You came down from where?"

"Let's just keep it simple. I'm here to help. Just know that, together, we can get the job done, because Noah and Annie love each other. No more fix-ups or introductions to new girls for Noah. Can I count on you, Mom?"

"Mom?" Rosalyn laughed. "Fine, but if this doesn't work, I'll be taking charge."

"Roz, honey, if this doesn't work, I'll be just a memory. I've got a lot riding on this. I love living here. Who wouldn't? You raised a great son and, if I might add, a terrific doctor. All his patients love him, even the crying ones."

"I couldn't agree with you more. His father's watching him with pride. So, what's the plan?"

"Don't know yet. Give me until tomorrow, and then we roll."

"Do we need Vera and Essie?"

"Nope, and you can't tell anyone about me. You hearing me talk needs to be a secret."

Rosalyn gestured that her lips were sealed.

Chapter Eighteen

Annie probably should have pretended she wasn't at home when Joseph showed up again, but she felt she owed him an explanation. She wasn't herself when they last spoke. His news had been such a shock that she barely remembered anything, other than asking him to leave.

"Can I come in?" Joseph asked, trying his best to be reserved. He didn't want to scare her off the way he had in his last visit.

From the way Annie opened the door to let him in, he could tell some of her resentment had dissipated.

"I wasn't sure you would let me in."

"I guess I was too upset to be understanding. This time, we can talk."

Joseph sat down on the sofa, and couldn't help but look around. He felt comfortable, and he really liked Annie. She was sweet and genuine, everything Francine had been when they were together. "I'm really sorry about our last visit," he began. "It's been a long time since I've had personal relationships. Meeting Rosalyn has changed my whole way of thinking. She's a big believer in family."

Annie smiled. "She's always been a great mother to Noah. Sometimes, she's a little over the top, but she was always a wonderful wife and mother, and a great friend. Without her help, I'm not sure what my life would have been like."

Joseph smiled, knowing that to be the truth. "I came here today to ask you to forgive me. I didn't mean to screw up your life. I only want the best for you. If you knew me, you'd know how much children mean to me."

"This isn't going to be easy for me either," Annie said.

"I know, but finding you has been a highlight for me. I just really didn't know how to act. I know business deals, not people. But, I want to learn to be someone you can count on. Can you give me a chance?"

Annie smiled sweetly. "I can do that. I wasn't exactly pleasant. I usually react better, but this just caught me off guard. Never in a million years would I have thought something like this was possible. I can learn to understand you, and you can do the same. It'll be difficult, because this is new for both of us."

Joseph sat back, a bit more relaxed. At least she wasn't asking him to leave.

"If Rosalyn can love you, I know you must be a good man. Oops, maybe I shouldn't have said that."

"It's okay. I've already told her how I feel. I'm in love with her. It's so unexpected, but wonderful."

"Would you like some coffee and cheesecake?"

Joseph smiled at his daughter. "I would love some. I've heard about your special blueberry cheesecake."

"I just happen to have some."

While Joseph sat there, he felt truly happy. Life had afforded him so many things, but finding out he had such a terrific daughter was the icing on the cake.

When Annie returned, Joseph took out a set of keys. "I have a surprise for you. I really thought about this, and I hope you'll accept."

"I'm not sure if I can take another one of these surprises."

"It's nothing like that. George, my driver and best friend in the world, is waiting in my car to drive you to Lake Geneva. I screwed up your mini-vacation last time, and I want to make up for it. This time, I think I'm giving you something you really need. A place to think."

"Really?"

"There are a few perks to being rich."

This time she laughed. "Guess so."

"It's my home. You can relax, listen to music, watch movies, anything you want. You can cook if you like; I know how much you like cooking. By the way, this cheesecake is incredible."

"Thanks, I do love cooking, but…"

"Molly can also come."

"How did you know that was my next question?"

"Because you love her, and this is your time. No one will bother you, but George will be on call if you need anything. What do you say?"

Molly came up to sit right beside her, and gave an excited bark. "Well, I guess that's your answer," Annie said. "We'll go. Thank you."

"No problem. I hope this is a good sign."

Annie gave him that smile he remembered. "Me too."

Chapter Nineteen

Noah finished his rounds earlier than usual, so he decided to take a run by Annie's apartment building. He didn't tell anyone, because he wanted to handle this himself. He didn't want Gracie's advice, let alone his mother's. Annie was the one he needed to see. If she just gave him a few minutes, he needed to tell her how he felt, and why she meant so much to him.

This was a new experience for him. What would he say? He was usually straightforward, but he was positive he couldn't just come out and say, "I love you." He also knew she might not talk to him at all. If Joseph hadn't come along and upset her, he would be with her now. Maybe he would tell her that, but maybe not.

He stopped at a flower shop on the way. He didn't know what flowers Annie liked, but he did the best he could. By next time, he hoped, he would know which were her favorites.

When she wasn't home, Noah was very disappointed. Right before he was ready to leave the flowers by the door, Wes stopped him. "You must be Prince Charming."

"I'm Noah Meyers."

Wes held out his hand. "I'm Wesley. The neighbor."

Noah laughed. "I know. Annie told me all about you."

"Really? She rarely mentions you, other than you're her boss. Just kidding. She loves your family, and how wonderful they were to her when she was young."

"What about me?" Noah asked, figuring the cat was out of the bag.

"What about you?" Wes was being coy, which wasn't his usual style. He needed to do what he could to pull this romance together. Not that it was his job, but Annie had become like a sister to him. "She doesn't say much about you."

Noah now felt a little uncomfortable. He had listened to Gracie for months, and was certain she wasn't wrong about their relationship. Standing there, he thought maybe she was; after all, she was a dog. Maybe he wasn't anything special to Annie. He loved Gracie, but she could be wrong.

That's when Wes began to laugh. "Hey man, I was just kidding. I shouldn't say this, but clearly Annie is a huge fan of yours. I think I know more about you than about Annie."

Noah smiled. "Really?"

Wes laughed again. "You straight men are all the same. You need to be hit over the head to actually figure out that you're in love. Anyway, if you're waiting here for Annie, you're going to be waiting a long time. She's in Lake Geneva. Joseph sent a car for her. She decided, what the hell, she was going to go."

"Do you know where she is?"

"Open up your hand."

"What?"

"Come on, man. Open up your hand."

"Fine." Noah opened his hand. Wes placed a set of keys into his palm, plus a piece of paper with the address. "There she is. Now go get her."

"I don't have my car. Now what? I'll go home to get my car. That should work. Right?"

"I know you must be a smart guy, because you're a very successful doctor. Just do yourself a favor and stop asking questions. The plan is in place."

"What plan?"

"Noah, get the hell out of here." Wes grabbed the flowers. "Thanks, I love flowers, so nice of you. Next time, get red roses."

As soon as Noah got outside, his car was there, and his mother was driving. Gracie was in the back.

"Mom, what are you doing here?"

"Picking you up and driving you to Lake Geneva."

"How do you know about this?"

Gracie shook her head. "Not me."

Noah knew Gracie must have had something to do with this, but he got in anyway, and Rosalyn started to drive.

"Wait," Noah shouted out. "Mom, there's no way you're driving. If you feel you must go, which I can tell is the case, I'm driving."

Rosalyn stopped the car and got out. "Okay, you can drive."

"I guess you both know where we're going. Am I right?"

"Noah, you're my son and I love you. But, this time, you're not the leader. You're being led."

When Noah looked in the rearview mirror, he saw Gracie nodding. "Great," he mumbled, "two Jewish mothers."

Chapter Twenty

Traffic was light, and it didn't take as much time as Noah expected to drive from the city into Lake Geneva. He had music on the entire time; this way, everyone chilled out and no one was giving him advice or opinions. It was terrific.

Noah was relaxed, deep in thought about what he was going to say to Annie. He didn't want to mention the office, because he needed to make clear that wasn't the reason he was there.

Rosalyn broke the silence. "You know we're not going to stay with you."

Noah was pleasantly surprised. "Really? That's good. When did you decide that?"

"A few days ago."

"So, you knew about this?"

"Sure did. It wasn't easy getting all the ducks in a row."

"Ducks…what ducks?"

Gracie answered. "Even I know that saying. It means everything…"

"Gracie why are you talking?"

Rosalyn laughed. "It's way past that point. I know she talks."

Noah took a deep breath. "Maybe this is all a dream, and I haven't gone completely mad."

Gracie jumped over and landed on Rosalyn's lap. "You're not crazy. You just needed a plan that worked, so I called for help. Guess what?"

"You're going to tell me, right?"

"Of course. By the end of today, everything will be just the way it was planned."

Rosalyn sat there, listening. It wasn't always easy for her to be silent, but she decided it was time to let nature take its course.

"Okay, Mom, what is it? You're way too quiet."

"I'm just thinking. You can't stop a girl from thinking."

Gracie looked right into Rosalyn's eyes. "Like I said, you need to trust me," the dog said. "This will work. It's about the magic of love."

Noah kept his eyes on the road, and stopped listening to the sideshow. He wanted to get everyone there safe and sound.

As they drove onto Joseph's property, Rosalyn couldn't help but be in awe. "Oh, my God. Maybe I've died and gone to Heaven. This place is spectacular. Right out of the magazines. Look at the grounds. The grass is green, and the flowers are vibrant. It's storybook style. Everything about this place is wonderful."

"Just for the record, we're not in Heaven," Gracie said. "Trust me. This is a beautiful place, but it's not Heaven."

As they pulled up, Noah glanced across the driveway, and saw Molly and Annie walking toward the car.

Gracie breathed a sigh of relief. "Noah, this is all for you. Don't let her wait too long. Before you go, there's one last thing you need."

Suddenly, a red rose appeared in his hand. "Where did this come from?" Noah asked.

"Don't you watch *The Bachelor*?" Gracie asked. "Now go. I'm sure you can figure out what to do when you get there."

Noah smiled. "I think I can take it from here."

From a distance, Rosalyn watched her son go to the woman he loved. As he handed Annie the rose, Rosalyn felt a chill in the air. She knew it was Ben. She looked up. "Thank you, honey. I'm not mad anymore. Our son found the right woman to love and share his life with."

Gracie inched her way closer to Rosalyn. "I think we've done our work. Let's get something to eat."

"Sounds like a plan," Rosalyn said. "Love always make me hungry."

"Well, Roz...I can call you Roz, can't I?" Gracie asked.

Rosalyn nodded and kissed the top of Gracie's head. "I don't see why not. You're like a grandchild to me."

"I don't think it works that way. Let's just say friends, and leave it at that."

"You know, I'm very persistent."

"So I've heard," Gracie said as she walked toward the house with Rosalyn. By the time they got to the house, Joseph was waiting outside, holding a red rose of his own.

Love is a wonderful thing, and you never know when love can happen, Gracie thought. *You just need to believe it will.*

The End

Other books by Marsha Casper Cook

Novels
Grand Central Station
Love Changes
Virginia Templeton Stories

Young Adult and Children's Books
To Life
No Clues No Shoes
The Magical Leaping Lizard Potion
The Busy Bus
Snack Attack
I Wish I Was a Brownie